The Dragon's Tooth

The Dragon's Tooth

by

Benjamin Coward

BC

Benjamin Coward
Gainesville, Florida, USA

ISBN 979-8-218-48152-0
First printing: 2024

Cover illustration by Ruth Bethea
Book design by Nancy R. Koucky, NRK Designs
Edited by Karin Nicely Lord, Seren Publishing Co., Inc.

BC

Benjamin Coward
Gainesville, Florida
USA

Thank you to my supportive wife, Julia,
and beautiful daughter, Annalise.

Prologue

THE WIND WHISTLED against the unyielding stone of the ancient granite walls. A grey dove glanced around, his head jerking rapidly as he took in his surroundings. The small bird inspected the dropped bread at his feet and quickly dipped to peck at it. As a large shadow moved over him, the dove jerked back upright, unfurling his wings to take off. But he didn't even have time to make a sound as the stealthy cat grabbed him by the neck and made a quick twisting motion. Watching the cat run off to a nearby alleyway with her prize, The Shadow smiled.

The attack had been perfect, and the look of shock and fear on the dove's face was exactly the entertainment The Shadow had looked forward to that night. Chuckling to himself, he thought of the symbolism in what had just occurred.

The Shadow turned, surveying his environs. The great city of Elizdiath had stood as the High Elves' capital and the Wizards' High Council headquarters for over a thousand years. With his efforts, however, The Shadow hoped that would soon change. Below him, the city sprawled out in all directions for six miles. A half mile away, on a hill a bit taller than his current vantage point, stood the High Elf castle, a great bastion of ornate stone towering into the sky with six magnificent spires. Even now, in the middle of the night, the glistening stone shone white.

His smile gone now, The Shadow turned back to his task. Before him rose the council building. Waiting for his cue, The Shadow stood hidden around the corner of the large but modest building, just close enough to the edge that he could see the entrance and hear anything occurring there. Its doors were large and imposing, made of solid, dark oak. On either side of the doors stood an elven guard wearing ornate plate armor embossed with rose gold in the shape of a blazing sun.

Not daring to breathe, The Shadow waited. He did not venture forth because of the stained-glass windows that he knew ran along the sides of the building. They were large—four feet across and nine feet high—each showing different and important scenes throughout the history of the world as they had been recorded by the wizards. The Shadow did not want the wizards to see him . . . at least, not yet.

Suddenly, hurried footsteps made The Shadow's heartbeat quicken with anticipation. His prey was finally here. A woman in a long, grey cloak ran up to the guards. Breathing hard, she lowered her hood slightly to show her face. Without question, the guards stood a little straighter as they hurried to open the door.

Excited now, The Shadow picked up the large rock he had brought with him, hefting the stone, testing its weight. He aimed and threw the stone over the two guards' heads to the opposite side of the building, where it clattered loudly on the cobblestones just out of the guards' sight.

The guards turned and walked towards the sound, with spears at the ready, while The Shadow turned back to the building and uncoiled a long rope with a cloth-covered grapple. Looking up, The Shadow gauged the distance to the nearest of the gargoyles that sat atop the building's corners.

With a quick and practiced motion, The Shadow threw the grapple over the gargoyle, where it made a muffled clink. The Shadow tested the grapple's hold and quickly ascended the building with long, lithe strides.

Now on the pitched roof, The Shadow hurried to the many moon-glass fixtures that looked down into the building below. As quietly as possible, he hurried to the one furthest from him. Through the window, he looked down into the council chamber, where ten wizards, from young adults to those far along in years, wore robes of blue and black and sat in mahogany chairs. In the middle sat a very old wizard with a full head of white hair that hung past his shoulders. Unlike the rest of the group, he wore robes of white trimmed in gold. Before the wizards stood the woman in the grey cloak.

She threw back her hood, revealing the face of a young, beautiful elf, her cheeks flushed from her haste to get there before it was too late. She was speaking hurriedly, arms and hands moving wildly, gesticulating at the old wizard before her, a pleading look in her almond-shaped eyes as she intermittently glanced back to the door to check that no one was coming.

The Shadow smiled and tested his rope, verifying that its hold was still sound. He then reached into his pocket and drew out a glass ball. Inside the ball, a deep-purple gas seemed to ebb and flow in circles like a huge summer storm coming out of the mountains.

Taking a deep breath, The Shadow stomped hard on the glass window before him, shattering it, and threw the ball into the room below. Everyone gathered there screamed. The old wizard looked up to the ceiling, making eye contact with The Shadow at last.

"No!" yelled the old wizard as he leaped to his feet, a large six-foot staff in hand. It was too late, though. The purple gas from the ball flowed upward, creating a portal through which came a multitude of goblins. The creatures ran forward with triumphant cries, their crude swords cutting down all in their path.

In response, energy balls and lightning came from the wizards who were still standing. Their assault dropped many of the goblins dead in their tracks.

The young elf woman screamed again, running for the exit, but a huge Kusarku came through the door of gas and grabbed the elf by her hair. The creature threw the elf to the ground, where she stayed, sobbing. The Kusarku was huge, with the upper body of a powerfully built man but the legs and feet of a bull. Two horns, each two feet long, protruded prominently from his heavy head, and deeply tanned skin covered his muscular, hairy body, decorated here and there with scars that spoke of past violence.

Suddenly, there was a commotion as the horde of goblins flung open the council building's front doors and poured forth into the street. Soon after, screams echoed up to The Shadow on the roof.

The scene calmed then, and The Shadow jumped through the broken window, gliding quickly down the rope into the building. The old wizard lay before him, the side of his head caked in blood, his wizard hat gone.

The old man looked up at The Shadow. "How could you do this? Your father would be ashamed to see you now," cried the old wizard.

"I do this for him and those too weak to get up off their knees," answered The Shadow, and he struck out hard with the toe of his polished boot, kicking the old wizard in the head, knocking him cold.

Goblins tramped forward, carrying the old wizard toward the purple gateway. The Shadow then turned to the elf woman still held on the ground by the large Kusarku, whose large hand gripped her white throat while a broad, evil smile played on his face.

The Shadow walked toward them, almost skipping with delight up to the elf woman. He looked down at her tear-soaked face. "Now then, what was so urgent that you wanted to tell them, sweet sister?" whispered The Shadow.

Chapter 1

CALDERON SIGHED, STOOD up, and stretched. He then looked at his handiwork. The trap he had set, a small, weighted snare, would be perfect for capturing the mountain deer he hunted.

Turning to look back the way he had come, Calderon shielded his green eyes against the last light of the spring day. He was a Kusarku, one of a race descended from minotaurs, with tan skin and eyes the color of new grass. He had two barely perceptible horns, coal-black and surrounded by raven hair that fell in cascades to his shoulders. His horns had always been a source of embarrassment for him as they were small and never seemed to grow much.

Calderon had a young face; he was sixteen, and stubble had begun to cover his chin, hiding a thin scar at the point of it. He had hooves for feet, but otherwise, he looked human. A dark tunic and comfortable pants suited him just fine, along with a small hunting knife in a well-used sheath. As always, he wore no shoes, his hooves being all he needed.

He scratched the scar with the back of his hand. When he was a young Kusarku out running at the edge of the Pyrite River, he had fallen on the slippery river rocks. He'd hit the rocks face first, his chin thudding on the unforgiving surface like the knock at an old door. He could still remember the shock of intense pain and then hurrying home, embarrassed and bleeding, with tears running down his face. Now, he moved carefully, like a cat on a fence.

Calderon glanced around as he stood. He was in a clearing near Eldall, one of the Gold Dwarf cities. However, he was far enough from the city to feel alone. He couldn't even see so much as a glimmer of torchlight from the many towers that surrounded the small but bustling city. The mountain air felt fresh and cool, and most importantly, free.

Lately, Calderon had felt cramped at his home in Dreadston Castle. Bard, his adopted father, had kept him shut up there, busy with one tedious task after another. After all his training and studies concluded for the day, all he did anymore was sit around the vast structure. With no news, no changes in the day-to-day tasks, and absolutely no risks, the boredom of it all was like a nail being driven into his fingertip. It was simply excruciating. He wanted to be useful and help, but how could he do anything locked up at home?

Calderon had set out a few hours before dusk and made his way to the clearing. A few years back, he had realized that deer frequently used this clearing as a path to the mountain lake, Aurum, where there was rich, green grass. He looked around on the Grey Mountain's forest floor, searching.

"Perfect," he said triumphantly.

Bending down, he picked up a fist-sized stone that fitted perfectly in his hand. Calderon had heard from many hunters that they had lost trapped prey to Night Panthers . . . or things much worse. And at times, he had been told grimly, the thieving beasts had taken more than just the hunter's prize.

Calderon looked around the clearing for a large tree from which to safely watch the snare. Off to his left, he could see through the trees to the shimmering surface of Aurum Lake. Spotting a large oak tree at least eighty feet tall and nine feet around, Calderon hurried over to it and began to climb, pulling himself up primarily with his hands, unable to find purchase easily with his hooves. The sap stuck to his skin and cloak as he went.

He settled on a large branch that overlooked the clearing. The branch was large enough that he could sit on it comfortably with his back to the tree's trunk. It was nice that even in troubled times like these, some things didn't change. You could always find peace in the mountain woods.

Calderon shivered at the thought of the only news that had recently come to Dreadston. Many races had been attacked, and each attack had always been instigated by an unknown leader. This was the case in the most recent attack, also, when goblins had suddenly attacked the elf capital of Elizdiath. What made this event even more disturbing was the rumor that a Kusarku had led the goblins in their assault. Because of this, the Kusarku and elven relationship had soured.

Fifteen years earlier, the Kusarkus had lost a huge portion of their people in the Grey War. They had also lost their king and queen— Calderon's own parents—the year after the war ended. For many of the Kusarkus, the deaths of Calderon's parents had been the final straw, and most thought that the tiny prince had died with his parents. For his own protection, then, Calderon had been raised by Bard, and the identities of his parents were kept a secret from most people. Had certain dissenters known he was still alive, his life would have been in grave danger. Instead, a tale was strategically spread that Calderon was the son of one of the king's guards who had died during the Grey War.

Calderon had grown up knowing how important it was to keep his parentage a secret. As the only child of the late king and queen, Calderon was the sole heir to the throne but too young to rule. As the king's best friend and chief councilor, Bard seemed the logical choice, so he became ruler in his stead. Not being of royal lineage, however, Bard was not crowned king but rather a minister to the people.

But the king's general, Krasp, had opposed Bard's rule from the beginning, and soon, this feeling only intensified. To Krasp's and many other Kusarkus' dismay and disgust, Bard had allowed the Kusarkus to fall under elven leadership, with the idea being that the Kusarkus would regain their independence when they could again stand on their own. Thus, the elves had become their "generous protectors."

"Damn elves," cursed Calderon softly.

The elves being their protectors meant that whatever obsidian the Kusarkus managed to mine, half of all the proceeds went back to the elves as payment for their "generosity and protection." Obsidian was the main source of export for the Kusarku kingdom. As miners, they weren't as skilled as the Red Dwarves or Gold Dwarves. However, the Kusarkus had spent generations refining and perfecting the making of weapons out of obsidian. The main reason most races didn't use obsidian was that it was so brittle. But the Kusarkus had found ways to get around this problem. After first chiseling the obsidian for smaller weapons like knives and arrowheads, or breaking apart larger chunks for larger weapons, the Kusarkus alone could deftly wield the magic to forge obsidian combined with metals into unique pieces renowned for their strength.

Now, the elves were sure to blame the Kusarkus for whatever happened in Elizdiath because … well, they had seen a Kusarku with the goblins. So, the elves could point their fingers at someone—especially someone who wasn't an elf—who could be controlling the goblins.

Isn't it bad enough that most Kusarkus who didn't die in the Grey War had fled and become little more than wanderers in the world? thought Calderon angrily. But that was Kusarku pride for you; they'd rather be alone and friendless than at someone's beck and call.

One thing was for sure, though: since the attack on the elves, there had been a stony silence from them. In an abundance of caution, Bard had forbidden Calderon from leaving the safety of Dreadston.

"To the fires of Flagrash with that," Calderon muttered under his breath.

Bard had taken care of Calderon most of his life. When Calderon was five years old, Bard had told him his parents, the young king and queen, had been brave warriors for their people and had died trying to protect them from harm. The thought that his parents had been such formidable warriors filled Calderon with pride, though he wished he could have known them. Bard didn't talk about them much. He said their loss was too painful to him, and Calderon never had the heart to force the matter.

Suddenly, a twig snapped, and Calderon hurriedly looked around. Across the clearing, he saw a tall man in travel-worn clothes, a longsword and battle ax crossed on his back. The man was walking at a careful, steady pace, looking around with the concentration of a cat looking for a bird. While most hunters looked at the ground searching for tracks or clues, this hunter was not. He was looking around in the air, which was saying something, for he was over six feet tall. Calderon thought he must just be lost; but what would a human be doing out here? So intent was the man's concentration that he was about to walk into Calderon's snare.

Taking careful aim with the rock still gripped in his hand, Calderon threw it just in front of the man. The man spun quickly around, his right hand flying to his shortsword on his back. Calderon jumped down from his perch in a spray of leaves and bark and threw his hands in the air.

"It's okay, friend. Just take it easy. I'm Calderon, and you're about to step on my snare," said Calderon as quickly and as calmly as possible.

The man's face relaxed, and he looked around the clearing slowly. "You said your name was Calderon, right?" asked the man in a hoarse voice. The stranger was about six foot two with brown hair, light brown eyes, and a stern face accentuated by a scar that ran down the right side, just missing his eye. "A minotaur, huh? Well, whatever. Just stay out of my way; I have business here," continued the man firmly but not unkindly.

Calderon walked closer, curious, choosing to ignore the use of his race's improper name. "And what are you doing so near Eldall?" he asked.

The man smiled ruefully. "What I am doing here and why is my business," he answered shortly. Then he grinned more widely. "Though, since we are being so formal and you don't seem to be a danger, my name is Duncan, and I am here hunting trolls," he said with apparent pride.

Calderon stared at Duncan, confused. Trolls in the Grey Mountains? Most trolls were in the Red Mountains, which hemmed the eastern side of the continent. And though it was rare, it was not impossible for trolls to come into the region of the Grey Mountains.

The Red Mountains met the Grey Mountains at the extreme north of the continent. The western side of the continent was where the Grey Mountains stood between the rolling hills of the main country and the great desert on the western side of Grey Mountains. As far as Calderon understood, most trolls that came to the Grey Mountains never stayed for long. The scenery and landscape of the Grey Mountains were apparently wrong—too many trees and too populated. The Grey Mountains were forest-covered. However, the Red Mountains where the Red Dwarves lived were more sparse and more suited for trolls.

Calderon looked up into Duncan's deep, dark eyes, eyes that told a long, sad story of living hard and most often alone. "If there is a troll here, does that mean that you are employed by the Gold Dwarves, possibly of Eldall?" asked Calderon.

Duncan cocked an eyebrow and said evasively, "Whoever is to pay me doesn't bother me. As long as I get paid, that's all I care about. As for what city we may be near, that doesn't have anything to do with me. I don't like cities too much or too many people."

Calderon thought he needed to tell Bard about the troll; this could be one more problem to add to the storm cloud that seemed to be hanging over their heads. So far as Calderon knew, the Gold Dwarves hadn't suffered attacks from "unknown sources." If Calderon brought news of this to Bard and it prevented trouble for the Gold Dwarves, then it could give the Kusarkus much-needed allies. Moreover, it showed how bad things were when the Gold Dwarves, with all their wealth, were having problems.

Calderon looked at Duncan and was about to inquire further when suddenly there was a noise in the underbrush on the left side of the clearing. Duncan's right hand again flew to his shortsword and silently drew it, ready for an attack. But Calderon did not want to cause any problems for his people by starting a fight without trying to first prevent it, so he gestured at Duncan for patience. Then, swallowing his fears and trepidation, he stepped forward and spoke in the direction of the footsteps.

"Hello! Who is there? We mean you no harm. Are you from Eldall?"

As Calderon finished speaking, both sets of footsteps (Because of course there would be two of them, thought Calderon) paused simultaneously then separated and began walking around the outside of the clearing. Calderon and Duncan got back to back, and Calderon drew his dagger with his right hand, while his left hand was thrust forward, ready to use magic. He was not yet as adept as he'd like at magic-wielding; however, he had been paying attention during his lessons with Bard. He was doing his best to continue to learn how to defend himself, to aid his guardian, and not to be seen as a child who needed protection.

Calderon noticed that though he couldn't see his quarries, he could tell their footsteps were very unsteady and unsure. Unsure because of the terrain? he wondered. Both the footsteps suddenly stopped and then began moving towards Duncan and Calderon.

After a moment, it registered with Calderon that he should be able to see whoever it was. If I can't see them, then they must be using magic, thought Calderon. He tried to detect the magic and thus sense where the enemy was.

Calderon concentrated, trying his best to remain calm and feel the magic around him. After a few seconds, he saw a faint silvery outline of a human-like figure that stood about four-and-a-half-feet tall. Putting confidence into his voice, Calderon said in Dwarvish, "I can see you. Give up, or I'll blow up the woods around you!"

There was a strange, rough laugh from both sides, and two dwarf-like figures appeared.

At once, Calderon knew that these were not like any dwarves he had seen before. They were less stocky and muscular, with dark, pitiless black eyes and hair and beard that were pure white and translucent. It was as though they had never even seen the sun before. The dwarf thing in front of Calderon drew a wicked-looking ax, let out a bloodcurdling war challenge, and charged.

From behind him, Calderon heard Duncan say under his breath, "Well, that is not good to see!"

There came another cry, though louder, from the dwarf behind Calderon, and then a loud metal-hitting-wood sound. A moment later, a tree fell where Duncan had been, making Calderon jump forward in fright. Duncan, he could hear, was charging forward.

Calderon had no weapon except his small hunting dagger. His only true defense was the little bit of magic he had learned. Focusing on his opponent with all his might, there was a crackle of electricity. Calderon concentrated on morphing the electricity into a ball. He could feel the sparks jumping between his fingers; it tickled. Calderon threw the ball of electricity. The magic hit the dwarf directly in the chest, and he was thrown, flailing, into the woods, where he hit a tree with a dull smack. A flurry of needles fell as he slid down to the base of the tree. There, the dwarf lay on the ground, not moving, sparking and smoking slightly, but still conscious.

Calderon glanced behind him to see Duncan standing over the bleeding body of the other dwarf, now disarmed. Duncan seemed uninjured, with his battle ax in one hand and his shortsword in the other. Both weapons were tinged in blood.

"Is he…" Calderon began to ask but broke off as Duncan looked up, his eyes blazing with excitement.

Through labored breaths, Duncan answered, "No, just unconscious. I didn't hit anything major—just flesh wounds. He grew in size and knocked down that tree there, but the way he moved seemed clumsy, as if he was unfamiliar with the area, giving me the advantage. Where's the other one?"

Calderon pointed to the tree where the second enemy sprawled.

"Magic?" Duncan asked.

In response, Calderon just smiled sheepishly. Duncan bent down, pulled his unconscious opponent over his shoulder and walked wordlessly with Calderon to the second dwarf, who was still slumped against the tree.

At their approach, the dwarf opened his eyes. Calderon's spell had burnt the dwarf's skin badly and had singed parts of his beard. As the dwarf tried to rise, he spat blood onto the ground at Calderon's feet.

"Who are you? Why are you here? Why did you try to attack us?" asked Calderon in Dwarvish.

The dwarf stared back at them with loathing in his eyes.

"Listen, just talk to us. I can help you. I might be able to save your life for the moment, but you have to talk to us," said Calderon, doing his very best to keep in control of himself.

The dwarf's only answer was to spit blood at Calderon's feet again. Calderon wanted nothing more than to be rid of both dwarves, but he knew his duty.

"Really, you're being too nice. Let me handle this," Duncan quipped, stepping forward and depositing the unconscious dwarf on the ground.

With an iron gaze, he began to draw his shortsword as he approached the second dwarf. Calderon stepped aside, hand raised to cast a spell if need be.

Duncan began to speak in broken Dwarvish: "If you don't want to end up like your sister over here, speak, or I'll do the same to you."

The Dwarf slowly raised his hands, both tightly clenched.

Duncan's shortsword arm relaxed, lowering the weapon slightly, and Calderon lowered his hand, releasing the grip on the spell he had ready. Mouth bloody, the Dwarf spoke quickly in an uncouth tongue. Calderon, and apparently Duncan, too, suddenly noticed a red glint in the Dwarf's right hand as he prepared to throw something. Both Calderon and Duncan leapt forward with no hope. Swiftly from behind them came two arrows, the first pinning the dwarf's wrist to the tree behind him.

The second arrow struck the dwarf, killing him instantly as it drove straight through his chest cavity and lodged in the tree behind him. Duncan leapt forward and agilely caught the red ball as it fell from the loosened grip of the now-dead dwarf. Calderon hurried over to where the arrows had come from. Concentrating hard, he lit up the area of woods with small floating lights. From the shadow of a large fir tree appeared Kyle, Calderon's best friend, his longbow in his left hand.

Calderon sighed with relief but allowed a look of annoyance to play over his face. Kyle gave him a sheepish grin. "It was a couple of good shots at least."

Calderon turned away and grinned despite his annoyance at being followed as though he were a youngling. Looking back over his shoulder, Calderon motioned for Kyle to follow him. Kyle, also a Kusarku, was a year older than Calderon and several inches taller, with a long, slender body. He had olive-green eyes and the tanned, tough skin of a farmer who knew a hard day's work. His dark brown, shoulder-length hair did not hide his horns, which were at least eight inches long already.

Calderon walked back to Duncan, who was staring closely at the glass ball in his hand. The ball seemed to be full of swirling fire. It was small—small enough that you could close your hand around it.

Thinking, Calderon asked Duncan, "Do you think it could be magical?"

Duncan looked at him quizzically. "I don't know much of any magic. I only know enough to get by. Why don't you have a look, kid?"

He gingerly passed the ball to Calderon, who set his mental focus on it, trying to see the ebb and flow of the magic.

Chapter 2

CALDERON WAS EXCITED, scared, and happy all at once. This was it—this was his chance at last after all the waiting. As he, Duncan, and Kyle ran, Calderon cleared his throat and said to Duncan, "So, you said you hunted trolls, but why, why would anybody hunt a troll alone?"

With his face expressionless, Duncan said, "It's just what I do."

Not to be brushed aside, Calderon asked again, "But why hunt a troll? I mean, it's a troll after all."

Kyle eyed Duncan keenly and commented, "I didn't think it was normal to hunt trolls alone,".

The dwarf groaned from Duncan's back, and without a second thought or breaking stride Duncan punched the dwarf in the nose, which began to bleed. The dwarf went limp again. Supremely unconcerned, Duncan appeared to be thinking hard then answered, "It's what I've always done. My father taught me to hunt trolls. He died on one of our hunts in the Red Mountains. My mom died when I was born, and my sister left when I was sixteen. And that's all there is." Duncan's face looked suddenly sad, and he asked, "Where are we going, anyway?"

"We are going to the Kusarkus' last castle, Dreadston," said Calderon.

Suddenly, Calderon was defensive. "Now, don't worry; there aren't many of us, and it is not like a big city. Most of our people saw the elves' control of our race as despicable even with the precarious situation we were in after the Grey War. Therefore, most Kusarkus are nomads. This is our last stronghold, the old castle of our beloved king and queen, who we lost fifteen years ago. My foster father, Bard, is the Regent of the Kusarkus."

Duncan's expression, which had been strained and almost worried, relaxed slightly. He frowned and said kindly, "I'm not one for history. I like to form my own impression of people rather than from rumors and gossip of ages past."

Calderon grinned to himself. It was refreshing to hear that at least some people didn't believe the rumors.

After a few moments of contemplation, Duncan asked hesitantly, "So, what do you call yourselves? I've heard many people say you are minotaurs. Is that correct?"

Calderon and Kyle both frowned, and Kyle burst out, "We are Kusarkus. To call us minotaurs would be to say we are beasts, like saying humans are just apes!"

Kyle continued to glower at Duncan, and Calderon cleared his throat. "It is correct that we are descended from minotaurs, but if you were to ever meet a true minotaur, our difference would be plain. They have less intelligence and are much bigger than we are. To call them beasts would be wrong, but they live alone and often attack anything that comes near them," explained Calderon calmly, hiding the fact that he, too, was offended.

The air was crisp and clean, and Calderon took a deep breath of it even though his lungs were beginning to burn with the exertion of trying to run in the mountains. Calderon could smell fresh pine needles dripping with dew drops. The early morning birds were beginning their greetings.

Duncan took a deep breath and loudly blew it out, a sparkle suddenly appearing in his eye. Through now labored breathing as they mounted a particularly large hill, he asked, "Is it true that your people make the only obsidian weapons? Are they really that great? I mean, from what I understand, they are just rocks. What's so special about them?"

Calderon thought he shouldn't tell Duncan everything, and indeed, Kyle gave him a guarded glance.

How the weapons were made was a secret. Small blades like knives and tips of spears could be made out of pure obsidian; to make swords, though, the blade had to be strengthened by other materials like steel and tungsten—and of course, a little magic never hurt. Calderon decided to Duncan a piece of the information but not all of it, a tactic he'd learned from Bard.

"Well, obsidian is actually volcanic glass, and when crafted correctly, it is much sharper than any other weapon, even those of diamond."

Duncan's eyes widened in shock.

Continuing, Calderon said with a bit of pride, "The Grey Mountains near here are one of the few places obsidian can be found because the mountains around here used to erupt and left the obsidian behind. The mountains don't erupt much these days, but there is still plenty of obsidian lying around. These mountains actually got their name because of the ash clouds that used to pervade the air."

"Also, from the fact that it rains here a lot," added Kyle, laughing.

Duncan and Calderon laughed, too, as a pine tree let fall a deluge of dew onto them.

Skillfully pulling out one of his arrows while not breaking his long-legged stride, Kyle allowed Duncan to see the black glass-like tip. Duncan remained silent, apparently either lost in thought or simply working to keep up with the two younger men as he had the added dead weight of the dwarf on his back.

After a while, they reached the top of a large hill. On the other side of the small valley before them was Dreadston. The castle was built into the mountain at its back for protection, so the outer wall only went around three sides, using the mountain for protection. Finally, they had made it. Calderon was breathing hard but glad they had made good time. He took in the castle and everything around them.

The four time-worn towers looked like fingers sticking out of the mountain, as though some giant hand was coming up from under the castle. Each of its towers was set on the point of a compass. The castle was made of solid granite, the same stone as the rest of the rock around it, but it was easy to see that Dreadston was falling into disrepair.

Worn down and being used mostly for storage, the south tower acted as a kind of gatehouse; it was the one closest to the main gate. The east tower held rooms for those who remained and worked in and around the castle, while the smallest west tower was where Calderon and Bard slept. Of the largest tower, the north, that was built into the very rock behind it, Calderon knew little save that it was where his parents, the king and queen, and their special guests had stayed. It had been shut since their deaths, a reminder of former glory.

Bard had been the king's right-hand man and had taken the loss of his monarch hard. However, he took over the "business" side of ruling, as Bard called it. Since the king's and queen's deaths, Bard had tried everything to keep the obsidian business alive though their population and supplies were always low. At first, therefore, the elves' help had been a welcome gift, but now things were changing.

Duncan had stopped dead, staring for a moment, his chest still heaving, his face wet with rivulets of sweat. Kyle stopped as well, taking an easy sigh and rolling his shoulders as though to loosen the tension there.

Old and worn though it was, the castle still it stood as strong as the mountains around it, stern and stubborn against the ever-changing.

"You said many Kusarkus live as nomads. I've heard this as well, but I never thought of how few of you were left," said Duncan in a melancholy voice.

Calderon nodded sadly. He had never seen what Bard called the "good old days," when the valley had been full of Kusarkus living in bustling houses all around the valley. He had heard there had even once been a kind of town square toward the east end of the valley where a small mountain river ran. Now, only a few ramshackle houses remained; the rest had been either destroyed by time from the harsh mountain weather or removed for the crop fields that ran in all directions.

Taking a deep breath of the pure mountain dew-filled air and giving Duncan and Kyle a reassuring nod, which they both returned, Kyle's accompanied by a wan smile on his face, they began their walk down into the valley. Duncan shifted the small dwarf on his shoulder, and

Calderon clapped Duncan on the back. Duncan was still looking nervous and uncomfortable.

Together they walked briskly in the predawn hours, the morning already becoming warm. They a few of the remaining farms and saw the crops—mostly leafy greens and root plants, like potatoes and turnips—just beginning to emerge from the ground. One of those houses was Kyle's, and indeed, Kyle glanced in its direction. No one was yet stirring in the houses they'd passed, but the trio could see lights in the sparse window slits in the castle before them.

Bard must be awake, then, along with the cooks, Calderon surmised. Bard always took pleasure in starting the day early and helping the cooks. He had once told Calderon, "You have done well when you can see others' appreciation; then you pat yourself on the back and keep moving. Start your day with something good, and your day will be good to you."

They had now reached the castle and Calderon turned to his companions. "Don't worry. It's going to be fine," he said to Duncan. "Bard is very congenial and fair. Just let me do the introductions."

Giving a jerky nod and stepping up with Calderon to the door, Duncan stood behind them, now looking relaxed. Calderon knocked on the massive, weathered double doors of dark oak with their polished iron knockers.

After a moment of uncomfortable standing on the doorstep, the door was opened by Bard himself, who had been concerned as to Calderon's whereabouts. Bard was tall and thin as a reed. His short brown hair and long black horns swept back in a Y formation. Bard's skin was pale, looking as though he rarely saw daylight. It was whispered by many that his mother had actually been a human or at least part human. Some also said this was another reason many of the Kusarkus had left: better to be on your own than follow a half-breed, they thought. Calderon hated the rumor; it only showed others' ignorance and resistance to change and the future.

Bard wore red robes that hung slightly loose on his frame. The Kusarku crest splashed across his chest a simple golden crown with flames in its center. He was middle-aged with a slight scar on his face from long-gone days when Bard had served the king. He had a kindly face, although presently, it looked tired and irritated with slightly bloodshot brown eyes.

Bard took in the three on the doorstep, looking first at Calderon, then Kyle, and then Duncan, and lastly, at the incapacitated dwarf.

Bard's eyes flew back to Duncan, and he frowned. Duncan, to Calderon's surprise, smiled. Something unreadable passed silently between them. Then Bard glanced away and wearily rubbed his eyes.

Without a word of greeting, Bard asked gruffly, "Calderon, what are you doing? Where were you? I was worried. And what in the Seven Kingdoms did you do to that . . . dwarf? Though, it doesn't look like any dwarf that I have seen."

Calderon hung his head, abashed. Duncan put the Dwarf down and Calderon quickly explained, his words spilling out, "This is Duncan. I was out hunting near Eldall when I ran into Duncan. He almost stepped into my snare. Then this Dwarf and another one attacked us. The other one died when he was shot by arrows from Kyle, who had been keeping watch nearby. The dwarf had been trying to throw this at us."

Calderon produced the glass ball of swirling fire and handed it gingerly to Bard. Bard took the magical sphere from Calderon, looked toward the castle doorway, and pointed sharply at the dwarf.

The left door was thrust open by Crackle and Lem, the door guards, who gave Calderon a quizzical look, grasped the dwarf under his upper arms, and carried him inside. Calderon looked back to Duncan, his eyes open wide, shocked by the abruptness of what had just transpired. Calderon then looked back to Bard.

Bard held the ball closely to him, his eyes transfixed upon it. Then Bard's eyes began to glow blue.

Calderon was confused; he didn't think Bard used magic. It wasn't exactly common, after all. Most of the races didn't have much magic, apart from the wizards. It was said that once, everyone had the ability to call on the ambient magic that existed around them. However, those times were past. According to what little Calderon knew about those times, the magic had been overused and abused, and although the wizards had tried to make magic abundant again, it was as King Adam once said: "You can't make something out of nothing."

Calderon was one of the few who felt the magic and could guide it, but he had no idea Bard could as well. Then suddenly, the blue glow disappeared, and Bard's eyes flew to Calderon, their gaze boring into him.

"You said you were near Eldall when you ran into the two dwarves?" asked Bard quickly with a stern look on his face.

"Yes," answered Calderon hesitantly as he wondered if a scolding was coming. But he hurriedly elaborated, telling in great detail all that had transpired.

Bard blinked and for a moment was apparently dumbfounded, then he looked between Calderon and Duncan. He paused, seemingly lost in thought, a curious expression on his face. Then he said slowly, "As you say, this could be a blessing for us. This could be the proof we need to prove our people's innocence, but we must work quickly."

Calderon knew what Bard meant. Since Duncan had been hired by someone to hunt trolls near Eldall, that "someone" was likely the Gold Dwarves. The trolls must have been attacking their city. And because Calderon had teamed up with Duncan to help protect Eldall, Duncan could now tell his employers that the Kusarkus were not the ones behind the attacks.

Suddenly exhausted, Calderon leaned against the wall and yawned. Kyle also appeared tired and cast a longing gaze toward his distant home and bed.

Bard gave Calderon a cold look that said, "You'd better get over it."

Duncan addressed Bard. "Well, as for me, I thought saving your son and helping out your race might get me some type of reward," said Duncan wistfully.

Bard gave Duncan a withering look. "I can understand a person of the road wanting to look out for himself, but everyone should try and help the other people who must live in this world, regardless. Each race is at each other's throat and threatening war because no one knows who is truly behind these attacks. We should all do whatever we can to prevent that, or we all will be affected," said Bard stiffly.

Calderon looked between the two—Bard, stiff and immovable; Duncan, curious and rueful. "So, what do we do? What do we do about Duncan? We do owe him for helping me," said Calderon, trying to break the awkward moment.

Bard's eyes softened slightly as he looked at Calderon. Apparently making some kind of a decision, he said, "Well, as part of a reward, take this," said Bard pulling forth his own pure obsidian dagger and its sheath from beneath his cloak and graciously handing it to Duncan. "This is some of our best work, and you will not find a sharper blade. And take this, too," continued Bard as he gave Duncan a small sack.

Duncan pulled out a gold coin and, after testing its weight, nodded and dropped it back into the sack. He then looked the dagger over and seemed very pleased as he put it back in its small leather sheath. Swinging his cloak over one shoulder, he attached the sheath and the coin bag to his belt.

As Duncan did this, Calderon caught a glimpse of several different religious symbols, both dwarf and human, that hung around the troll hunter's neck.

"Now then, as for a plan," continued Bard, "I want you, Duncan, to take the strange dwarf you apprehended to Alezadria, the human capital, and bring him before King Adam. I will write a message for the king in hopes that he will assemble a council and bring all the races together to discuss the fact that two dwarves of some kind were found with a powerful weapon so close to Eldall—and that you and Calderon stopped them. My hope is that you will remain in the human city to be able to bear witness to what you and Calderon saw and did. Once we receive a letter from Adam asking Calderon to come to the city for the council, I will send him after you."

Throughout all this, Duncan nodded, a little dazed but not appearing displeased at the thought of more riches.

Calderon, on the other hand, was fuming; he had helped bring all this about, and now he was to just sit idly by and wait to play messenger while Duncan went to tell his side of the story first. "Father, I want to—" began Calderon angrily but broke off when Bard gave him an irate glare out of the corner of his eye.

"Duncan, if you will follow me, I can show you a map that will lead you in a quick route to the castle," said Bard, motioning for Duncan to come in. Duncan nodded and offered a smile, which Calderon returned half-heartedly. Then the two walked off through the main hall and into Bard's small study off the east side of the main hall.

Calderon nudged Kyle. "Why don't you run home and catch a few winks? I'm sure Bard is going to want to talk for a while."

Kyle laughed easily and slapped Calderon on the back, making him wince. "I'll let you fill me in later on what Bard says," said Kyle, running off, his hooves clopping on the hard dirt.

Calderon walked into the main hall, which was empty at the moment but for Crackle and Lem, who stood beside the dwarf. The prisoner's wounds had been tended to, and he was sitting up now, restrained by heavy iron chains and manacles and securely gagged. At that moment, Crackle looked around and waved for Calderon to come over. Crackle nodded to Calderon and asked tersely, "Could you guard the dwarf with Lem? The human needs a horse and provisions."

Crackle was a swarthy Kusarku in his late twenties with red hair and skin the color of bronze. He wore a simple chainmail shirt that hung loose on his tall, lanky frame.

Calderon nodded, and Crackle hurried off to see to his duties.

Lem let out a sigh. He was a muscular Kusarku of average height. He had blond hair and brown skin with horns that were over a foot long. He, too, wore a chainmail shirt and a longsword on his hip. In a deep voice, he asked, "So, what in the Seven Kingdoms happened?" Lem was always gruff but very kind and caring. He had quite a few times sparred with Calderon when Calderon was young, instructing him in the practical art of swordsmanship.

Calderon grimaced and told Lem of the attack and how Duncan had helped.

Lem winced. "Magic. Didn't I always tell you that using those devil arts was no good?"

Calderon frowned. "But it saved my life this time," he said defensively.

Lem grumbled to himself and gave the dwarf at his feet a look of hatred and disgust. The strange dwarf, as he had for the last few minutes, continued to curse at him through his gag.

Calderon looked around the room. Cooks and other servants were now moving through the great hall, coming down from the west tower where many of the people in the castle lived. They gave Calderon and the dwarf curious looks as they went to start the day's tasks.

Lem broke the silence. "What is this thing?" he asked, indicating the dwarf. "I've seen many dwarves before and lived in the mountains all my life, and I've never seen a creature like this."

Calderon shrugged. "I don't know, and I don't think I've read anything about these in my studies in Alezadria."

Then there was a commotion, and Calderon looked up to see Bard emerging from his study with Duncan, who was looking at a folded piece of paper in his right hand. As he walked toward Calderon, Duncan slid the paper inside his grey cloak.

Bard seemed more relaxed, now, as he rejoined Calderon. He put an arm around his foster son and spoke in a low but kindly voice in the young man's ear. "We will talk soon. There is much we need to discuss."

Together they all walked through the main doors. Outside, they met Crackle, who held the reins of a large bay horse.

"Inside the bag are enough provisions to more than get you to Alezadria," said Bard to Duncan.

Lem draped the still-cursing dwarf over the back of the bay. Duncan nodded, his face impassive, then looked at Calderon. Clapping him on the back, he said, "I'll see you there soon. Just make sure you don't take too long." With a final wave and sly smile, Duncan turned and rode off with the dwarf bouncing, his grunts of protest unheeded, behind him.

Chapter 3

As Calderon stood with the others watching Duncan's form disappear into the growing light of morning, he turned to Bard. "Why do I need to stay until we get word?"

Bard's expression remained unreadable as he turned back to Dreadnot and beckoned for Calderon to follow him into the castle. Inside, there were even more inhabitants up and about. Lefe, the stocky, broad-backed blacksmith in his middle years, hurried across the hall to his forge, likely to begin on the next round of obsidian weapons. Malvin, a local farmer, was yawning in the far-right corner, alone, trying to recover from his night's drinking. Two of the assistant cooks, Karen and Kasey, scurried in with a trays full of dishes prepared for the people coming down for breakfast. All barely looked up at Bard and Calderon crossing to the west wing of the castle.

Bard and Calderon next walked along a dark, dank hallway, lit only with torches, until at last, they came to the end, where it turned left toward the hospital and armory. Straight ahead stood the west tower, and on the right, a large oak door, which Bard opened.

Bard had not spoken at all to Calderon as the two filed into the room and Bard closed the door behind them. He crossed the small room and sat behind his massive desk, made of a dark pine and covered with papers. The room was full of similar stacks of papers, Bard's idea of organization. On the wall behind Bard was the Kusarku coat of arms on a red-and-black banner. Along one wall sat several heavy trunks. Leaning against one of these was Bard's primary weapon, a finely made rapier, its silver basket hilt designed to curve cage-like around the wielder's hand, protecting it from harm during combat.

Bard sighed and stretched; he seemed very weary. He turned his focus to Calderon and spoke at last. "Calderon, I do understand how you have been feeling cooped up here. It's hard for me to say this, but the time has come for you to be a man and embrace the position you have been trained for."

Calderon tried his best not to roll his eyes. He suspected another lecture on being responsible for his actions was next.

Bard continued, "With all this in mind, how could you be so foolish to go to the Grey Mountain alone? What if things had not gone your way? Where do you think you would have been then? You could be dead, along with many of the Gold Dwarves who could have been attacked, and we would be none the wiser as to what had happened to you!" At the last word, Bard slammed one hand down on the table, scattering a nearby stack of papers.

Calderon looked down, abashed. He had not thought about it like that. He felt his cheeks grow hot with embarrassment and his eyes sting with frustration. Bard gave Calderon another long look, which Calderon did his best to meet but, in the end, failed miserably, finding himself examining his hooves. A thought then occurred to Calderon, and he looked up hopefully.

"What did you mean when you said Duncan was to have Adam send word to us for me to come to a council?" asked Calderon.

Bard stood up, clearly agitated, and began to pace the room. "What I meant," said Bard, "was that I want you to go to Alezadria and speak for our people. You need to stand as a witness, along with Duncan, to what occurred. It could show the other races that the Kusarkus are looking out for them, not trying to wage war on them. This could save many lives if it goes well. Adam has claimed his support, but we will need the trust of all the races if we hope to stop a war."

Calderon had not realized the importance of what he and Duncan had done. And now he would get to go and relay his tale in front of King Adam and hopefully those of importance from the other races. His heart was racing; he had been waiting for such a chance. But suddenly, he felt a pang of doubt. What if he failed? What if he could not convince the others that the Kusarkus were not behind the attacks?

Calderon, still seated, looked up to find that Bard standing next to him. The older Kusarku put a hand on his adopted son's shoulder.

"Cal, I believe in you. Our people couldn't be in more capable hands. But you need to think through your actions because they could have far bigger repercussions." Bard paused as if steeling himself, then he nodded.

Bard turned and walked over to the wall where seven cedar chests sat. Six of the chests were large, at least six feet long and secured with heavy iron locks. These were organized in two stacks, each three chests high. Sitting atop those, the seventh chest was only about three feet long, but it was wrapped with a large iron chain with three iron locks on it. The smaller box, Calderon noticed, bore a sigil of a morning glory.

Bard slid the small box over and then, with discernible effort, took the top right chest down and put it on the ground behind the desk.

Calderon couldn't see exactly what Bard was doing as he bent down, but Calderon thought he heard the familiar clink of the keyring Bard always kept in his pocket. Next, there was the click of a lock and the squeak of a hinge.

Bard straightened up with another box in his hand. This box was well polished, made of mahogany, and was about four feet long. Bard walked over to Calderon and placed the box in front of him on the desk, sending several more papers to flutter to the floor like falling leaves.

Bard looked at Calderon with a sober expression on his face. "I know we haven't talked about your parents much, but I know they would be proud of you if they could see the man you have become."

Calderon's heart beat faster. His whole life, he had wanted to know more. What could be hidden in this box? Calderon wondered. Could it be letters from them? Or clothes? Or some family heirloom?

Bard opened the box.

Calderon walked over to stand beside his foster father. Inside the box was a sword, but it was unlike any he had seen before. The sword was short, very short; it was like a shortsword with an overly large hilt and grip. It seemed to be made to be held in two hands. Its blade was the glossy black of obsidian, and a ripple effect ran down its length. The sword's hilt was wrapped simply in leather, just like its crossguard. At the end of the hilt, a thin chain was attached, and on the other end of the chain was a thick steel clasp. Calderon looked at the weapon in wonder. He had neither seen nor heard of one like this one.

His voice low and sad, Bard said, "This was your father's. He left it in my care before he died. It was very precious to him, and he and your mother never thought anything would happen to them, especially not an ambush."

Calderon's brow furrowed. "But why leave the weapon behind if it was so good?" he asked.

Bard's face hardened. "I said he left this weapon in my care. I never said he went off unarmed. Your parents were many things, but they were never careless, and it's not up to us to question their motives."

Humbled, Calderon dropped his eyes back down to the blade.

Suddenly, a question occurred to him. "How exactly do you use this . . . weapon?"

Bard quirked an eyebrow at him and grinned slyly. "I leave that up to you to figure out. All I'll say is don't hold it by the pointy end."

Calderon slowly reached down and gripped the weapon's hilt. As he touched the leather, Calderon thought he saw flames running along the blade, making it seem like the ripples moved. Then Calderon blinked, and the fire was gone. He lifted the blade; it was very light, and he moved it effortlessly, but because of the chain weighing the sword down, the balance of it was off. Calderon wondered what the chain could be used for as he picked it up and slung it over his left shoulder. Then, he sheathed the sword in a plain black-leather scabbard, which had been in the box beneath the weapon, and attached it to his belt.

"For now," Bard added, "I'll see to it everything is ready for your departure. I'll need to strengthen security and castle defenses as well. It could be even more important that the council goes well—if so, we could ask the Gold Dwarves for assistance should we be attacked. Also, before you leave, I might have one more thing for you. I'll have it brought to your bedchamber when it's ready".

Calderon nodded and walked to the door. "I'm sorry, Father, for worrying you. I'll do better in the future," said Calderon. He reached for the door handle, and behind him, Bard cleared his throat. Calderon turned back to see Bard, misty-eyed and appearing twice his age as he leaned against his desk.

"I know you will. Just don't forget your parents and I love you."

Calderon, not knowing what to say, simply nodded and pushed through the door.

Calderon walked in a daze to the main hall. He was starving, of course, but inside, his head was full of buzzing. He had his father's sword—his sword! With my father's own sword, I can prove myself, thought Calderon. It was like having a part of him, and knowing that his father had treasured the weapon was mind-blowing.

Also, what was that about an ambush? As far as Calderon knew, no one knew what had happened to his parents.

With so many thoughts running through his mind, he didn't even register all the inhabitants of the castle now eating while staring at him.

Calderon walked over to the far corner of the room, drew the sword, and put it and the chain in front of him on the table. Still in awe of the blade's rippled pattern, he stared at the beautiful weapon. When he'd touched the hilt this time, however, he hadn't seen the weird flames that had appeared before. It must have been a trick of the light, Calderon thought, adding to the fact that he was exhausted.

"Excuse me, Cal."

Calderon jumped and looked around to see the youngest kitchen and serving maid, Molly, standing at his elbow. He had not even noticed her approach as he had been so engrossed in looking at the sword.

"Yeah, Molly—sorry. Could I get a small bit of breakfast?" asked Calderon.

"That's just what I was going to ask you." Molly smiled and blushed. She was a year younger than Calderon but very pretty with brown eyes, brown hair, and dark skin. Calderon had always been rather taken with her and hoped he hadn't hurt her feelings as she hurried off. As Calderon watched her go, he hoped Kyle had never noticed the looks he shot at her.

Calderon looked around the room and saw Kyle hurrying up to him with his longbow and a quiver of arrows on his back. Kyle's horns, as ever, seemed to shine. He was sure that Kyle polished them. Calderon wondered if having horns like Kyle's gave you a headache.

Kyle sat down across from Calderon, putting his bow and quiver down on the table as he said ruefully, "Dad was pissed, as always. Well, whatever."

Calderon put down his head and smiled in spite of himself. "You were right that I shouldn't have gone, but you should hear what Bard said," said Calderon, who then told Kyle in a hushed voice everything that had happened.

Kyle stayed quiet throughout the story, and when Calderon finished, he sat back, his face impassive. Calderon frowned at his friend's lack of enthusiasm.

Just then, Molly hurried back over and deposited two plates in front of the young Kusarku. At the same time, she moved Kyle's bow and quiver off the table, giving him a look. Calderon moved his own weapon off the table and onto the seat beside him. He then thanked Molly for the meal. Molly smiled and hurried off again; Calderon couldn't help but notice the way her hips moved as she walked away.

Kyle leaned forward and grinned. "So, when do we leave?"

Calderon frowned. "I can't take you with me. I'd never forgive myself if something happened to you."

"Take me with you, or I'll follow you. You know I'm a better tracker than you," answered Kyle stubbornly.

"But what about your family and your plans to enter the Archers' Guild?" asked Calderon. The Archers' Guild was a selection of the best archers in the land, chosen from all the races. They patrolled the land and helped each race in times of need. Calderon knew Kyle had always dreamed of joining the guild, and as their best archer, Kyle had a great chance of being chosen as a member.

"My family will be fine, and my resume will be even better if I help you. The Archers' Guild will still be there when this is all over."

Calderon smiled. If he was honest with himself, he had not liked the idea of traveling all the way to Alezadria alone. "All right, all right. I'll ask Bard's permission for you to go. But don't forget you will have to convince your parents."

The two started eating the eggs and bacon Molly had brought them. After a few minutes, Kyle broke the silence. "You said you need to practice with your new sword, right? I say we go train after we are finished eating".

Calderon nodded his agreement, his mouth still full of egg, and saw Bard enter the room, walk over to Darm, and start talking. Darm was the eldest Kusarku. Veins ran through his mottled skin like mountain rivers. He had very long, thin horns and walked with a cane and a pronounced limp. It was said that Darm had been a teacher in his younger days and that he had instructed both the king and queen as well as Bard. These days, Darm told stories of the old times, legends near and far, and fairy tales like those of the mythical Dragon's Tooth. Calderon was wondering what the two could be talking about when Kyle brought him out of his thoughts.

"How exactly are we going to get to Alezadria without elves or someone else stopping us? I mean, it wouldn't be the first or the last time our people were attacked on the road just for being ourselves, and these aren't exactly peaceful times."

Kyle's words held a nervous edge. His parents were farmers, and though Kyle had been to many places in the Grey Mountains, he had never been outside the region before. Many of the Kusarkus were of similar mind. Even those who were nomads rarely left the supposed safety of the Grey Mountains. There had been an increased fear of being persecuted, and many believed the mountains helped to shield them.

Kusarkus were on good terms with both dwarf clans. All three groups had many similar interests, so they tended to get along, but with other races, not so much—especially the elves.

"Bard will come up with a safe way to get us there, and remember:

I trained there, so I know my way around," said Calderon, doing his best to sound reassuring while swallowing his own fears.

Kyle didn't seem entirely convinced, but he let the subject drop.

Changing the course of the conversation, Calderon pulled his father's weapon up on the table again and showed it to Kyle. "I still can't believe it. Have you ever seen a blade like it?" said Calderon in a hushed voice.

Kyle bent forward and inspected the blade and chain, a puzzled expression on his face. Finally, after a minute, Kyle spoke. "It's weird, that's for sure. Why have the chain, and what are those ripples for?"

Calderon shrugged. "I don't know, and like I said, it's going to take practice to learn how to use it." Kyle leaned forward again, frowning. "The blade does not look like our obsidian blades do. What could it be made of?"

Calderon frowned as well. Kyle was right—the blade was a shiny black even darker than the obsidian blades they forged. It was such an alien weapon.

Shaking his head, Calderon sheathed the weapon. "Well, shall we get some training in and figure things out? I'll bet I can beat you out to the training yard," said Calderon, springing to his feet.

Kyle jumped out of his chair, too, and the two sprinted out the west archway, ignoring the looks they got from the others around them. On the other side of the room, Bard smiled. Everything was working out so far, but he had to be sure. Excusing himself from Darm, Bard made his way to the west tower to watch.

Chapter 4

Calderon stepped back from his practice dummy. It was so frustrating. Each time he swung the sword, the blade always hit either a few inches from his mark or off angle. Calderon knew that such inaccuracies, in real combat, could mean his death. The blade cut very deep, though, and he would soon need a fresh dummy. This one already had the head gone, and the stomach area was barely holding the straw in anymore. He wiped the sweat from his brow. Holding the thin, six-foot-long chain rolled up on one shoulder while trying to fight normally was an arduous task. Across the training yard, he heard the dull thumps of Kyles' barrage of arrows, each striking with deadly accuracy.

Walking over to a second dummy, Calderon took a ready stance. He danced forward, swinging the sword in an upward cut across the midsection, spilling straw everywhere. He pulled back and then jumped forward, stabbing all the way through the dummy's chest and out the other side. As the blade had moved without resistance through the dummy, Calderon toppled forward. He sat on the ground and cursed. Hearing footsteps, he turned his head to see Kyle walking toward him.

"Are you hitting the dummy, or is the dummy hitting you?" teased Kyle, holding out a hand and pulling Calderon to his feet.

Calderon scowled, "I just can't get it. The chain is throwing everything off." Calderon stomped a few steps away from the dummy and threw the sword point first at the figure's head, where it buried itself up to the hilt. Calderon pulled the sword free and stormed off.

Kyle caught up to him and patted him on the back. "Maybe you aren't supposed to hold the chain on your shoulder. What if you let the chain hang from your belt or from your back? Why don't we go ask Lefe? He might have some ideas about it."

Calderon nodded, ashamed of his outburst, and the two of them walked off toward the smithy on the far side of the training area, where they could already hear the steady banging of the forgemaster.

Bard watched the two leave the training yard, a frown on his face. Calderon would need to learn fast, and throwing a temper tantrum did nothing to further their cause. Then something caught his eye. He hurried down to the training yard and up to the dummy Calderon had thrown his father's sword at. Where the blade had pierced the material was a singed hole, as though the metal had been white hot and had burned away the cloth and straw around it. Bard's frown turned into a jubilant smile.

"Calderon, you are definitely your father's son," said Bard. He turned and hurried back inside with a skip in his step and whistling a merry tune.

The forge was swelteringly hot. Lefe, shirtless but for the leather apron he wore, worked at an anvil on a three-foot long rough piece of obsidian. As the Calderon and Kyle entered the shop, Lefe looked up from his work and quickly held up a hand, indicating for them to wait. He quickly finished hammering down the sword's length and put the blade into the fire behind him. Then he sat down on his small well-worn seat. He mopped his dripping brow and beckoned for them to come closer.

"Work those bellows for me, Kyle," said Lefe. Kyle hurried over and began pumping quickly. "Slower! You will weaken the blade if the fire is too hot," Lefe added sternly. "Anyway, what can I do for you two?"

Calderon looked at Kyle, who was beginning to sweat but gave him a nod to go on. Calderon handed the sword toLefe and said, "I need to know the best way to keep this chain out of my way while fighting. I don't want to have to hold it all the time. It throws off my balance."

Lefe looked at the weapon and frowned.

"Well, if I were you, I'd just work on my strength," said Lefe.

"But—" Calderon started to say, but Lefe held up a hand and continued.

"If you were to put the chain on some type of attachment, then you would take away its use and might as well take the chain off the blade. You should think outside the box about how the chain could be beneficial to you."

Calderon stared at him incredulously. "But if I were to throw the sword at people and it didn't hit, then they could just block my throw and I'd be defenseless," argued Calderon.

"I never said you should not use your brain. You do have one, you know. And there is more than one way to do things. However, here—use this when not using the weapon." He picked up a piece of leather and walked over to Calderon. With a grumble, he kneeled down at Calderon's side. When he sat back up, the leather was wrapped around Calderon's belt with a button at the top. "There. That can hold the chain. Now, get out of here. The blade is hot enough, and if I wait any longer, it will not be strong enough to block off blows."

Dejected, Calderon turned, and he and Kyle left the smithy to the renewed sounds of steel on obsidian.

Calderon sat down in the grass of the empty training yard, fuming. He laid his father's sword in front of him and stared at it, trying to think. What role could a chain play in fighting?

Kyle sat down as well, drawing his knees up to his chest. "At least the sword is sharp," he commented.

Calderon nodded absently. He hated being stumped by a problem.

After a few minutes of silence, Kyle asked, "What do you think that thing was? I mean, it looked like a dwarf.

Calderon nodded. "It was smaller, though, and not as muscular as most dwarves. Their eyes were pure black, and their hair was all white— and you could see right through it."

Kyle frowned. "Makes you think of the old stories Darm tells of changelings, dunkles, dvergar, and fairies." Kyle laughed and lay back, looking at the clouds.

But Calderon's mind was buzzing. What if those things were dvergar or Dark Dwarves? It was said that ages ago, before the Red and Gold Dwarves had split into two separate entities, there had been another group of dwarves, the Dark Dwarves. It was said that they lived deep under the ground, so deep that light was never seen. They were said to be cruel and malicious. The Dark Dwarves had repeatedly attacked the other dwarves, stealing the dwarves' work, and what they didn't steal, they destroyed. Finally, the other dwarves had led an attack against the Dark Dwarves, routing them, and the Dark Dwarves were never seen again. Or were they?

"What if they were Dark Dwarves?" asked Calderon.

"And what if I could fly?" answered Kyle, laughing. "You're kidding yourself, Calderon. Even if they were once real, they are not now. The other dwarves made sure of that."

Calderon lay back, too, still lost in thought as the clouds went by. After a few minutes, Kyle got to his feet and picked up his bow.

"Well, I'd better go break the news to my folks about going with you. Make sure you get some rest, though, Calderon. You look terrible."

Calderon gave him a wan smile, and Kyle waved and made to leave but tripped over the sword's chain, his hooves tangling in it, and he fell to the ground. Calderon quickly helped free Kyle's hooves, laughing at his friend's curses. Kyle got himself upright again and walked off, muttering to himself.

Calderon laid back again on the soft grass, still laughing, then a thought occurred to him, and he quickly sat up. What if he used the chain as not only a way to increase his reach but also as a distraction or a trip hazard for his enemies? Of course, it would have to be perfected. The only way to do that was to work with the chain and make his arms stronger, so he sat up and tried to come up with moves he could use in battle. One was throwing a length of the chain at the legs of an enemy then quickly jumping in with a slash or stab. Soon, Calderon was breathing hard. As he turned back to the castle, he saw Bard standing in the doorway there. Calderon walked over to him, sheathing his sword, wrapping the chain up, and attaching it to his belt as he went.

"You know, your father would do a very similar move in battle. Just keep practicing, and I'm sure you will be as good a fighter as he was," said Bard.

Calderon grinned. "It's tough to get the hang of, but I'm starting to get some ideas," he said, happy at the praise.

"Anyway, why don't you get cleaned up and take a rest. I wouldn't want you to make a mistake. I'll wake you before dinner," said Bard as he turned and walked back into the castle.

Calderon made his way to the east tower, snagging an apple and some bread from the kitchen as he passed and receiving an angry look from the old cook, Joan. Calderon climbed the curled stairway to the fourth landing, where he pushed open a small oak door. Once inside, he closed the door, leaned against it, and took a large bite out of the apple he had taken. The apple was sweet and juicy and made a satisfying crunch as he bit into it.

Calderon's bedchamber was sizeable but somewhat dark and modestly furnished. A heavy cloth covered the window, and a small but comfy bed stood in the left corner. The rest of the room was taken up by knick-knacks—small knives; diminutive likenesses of many forest animals, which he had meticulously carved; and stones of all colors, polished smooth by mountain rivers.

Against his bed leaned his falchion. Someone, most likely Bard, had brought it up for him. Calderon remembered having left it at the training yard the day before. He had stormed off, frustrated at being cooped up.

He set the bread and apple on his bed then neatly placed his father's sword on the large cedar clothing chest at the foot of his bed. He put a hand on the sword one more time and turned away. Calderon crossed to the window, removing his leather jerkin and linen shirt beneath as he went. He threw aside the cloth that draped the window and bent down to the cool bowl of water on a small table and washed himself. When he was finished, he pushed his wet hair back and dried himself with a towel.

Calderon stretched, looking out to the valley below, which was now busy with activity. Yawning and closing the shade of his window, he crossed to his bed. He lay back, taking a few more bites of the apple and bread, which he quickly finished. Putting the remains of the apple on his bedside table, Calderon again lay back and closed his heavy eyes. He was just thinking there was no way he could sleep when he drifted off.

When Calderon awoke a few hours later, it was still light out. His body was sore all over. He stretched and pulled on a loose-fitting tan shirt. On his belt, he put his favorite hunting knife. He couldn't believe he had forgotten it.

"What would I have done if I'd actually caught a deer? Bard and Kyle were right, as always. I didn't think that through," he muttered, chastising himself. Calderon left his bedchamber, closing the door behind him, and groaning at his aching joints as he went down the tower stairs.

The main hall was quiet with the majority of the castle's residents out doing their daily tasks.

"I'm no use to anyone," Calderon said with a sigh. He sat down in the middle of the empty hall and looked around. Then, something caught his eye. At the other end of the hall, the large oak doors to the throne room were slightly open. Curious, Calderon crossed the space and entered. The throne room, built into the mountain behind the castle, was dark and naturally cold.

At the other end of the room knelt Bard, facing the two stone thrones. Behind the thrones, there was a huge scarlet tapestry emblazoned with the Kusarku coat of arms. Bard's head was bowed. Calderon couldn't see his face, but from the slump in his foster father's shoulders, he could tell he was sad. As Calderon made his way through the empty throne room, his hoofbeats echoed off the walls. Bard stood up and turned at the sound. He nodded to Calderon and beckoned for the young Kusarku to follow him. Bard led him through a small oak door behind the thrones.

Inside were two polished marble sculptures of the king and queen. They were life-size, and their heads were together, looking down at a bundle in the queen's arms. King Torin was handsome with shoulder-length hair and a short beard. His horns were short, and he had the muscular build of a warrior. He was dressed in scale mail, but the expression on his face was full of kindness and compassion. Queen Elaine was beautiful with long hair and short horns curved almost into spirals. She was also dressed for war, her right arm holding the small bundle and her left hand on a lance at her side.

Calderon looked at Bard. "I've never seen this before. You said they died bravely, right?" asked Calderon.

Bard nodded. "It was a day I'll never forget. I thought you should see them, though. Your father once told me: 'I don't fight for a man or a country; I fight for hope and love.'"

Calderon nodded, his eyes stinging. Looking at the visage of his parents for the first time in a while, he realized some might call him, Calderon, a prince. It made him uncomfortable; he didn't deserve that and didn't think he could ever begin to measure up to what would be expected of such a station.

"What were they like? I mean, I know what people say, but you were close to them," said Calderon quietly, trying to take his mind off his thoughts of responsibility.

"Torin was brave and proud and an amazing strategist. He was also the best friend I ever had," answered Bard just as quietly, his eyes on the statues. Bard continued, "Queen Elaine was a true lady with a smile and laugh that could truly light up a room. She always seemed to give good advice and was always there to support me or Torin with wisdom or comfort."

Bard patted Calderon on the back, and the two left, closing the door behind them. As they made their way across the hall, Calderon asked, "Do you ever think about them? Or what they would do now?"

Bard answered with a sad smile, "Every day, but we have to do the best we can without them. And they wouldn't want us to be lax."

Calderon spent the rest of the day reading books about spells. Dreadnot castle didn't have many spell books, and most of these were old and full of religious rhetoric of the great fire. It was once believed—and some still did believe—that the Kusarku race came from a great fire. Fire was the great destroyer and the great life bringer. They believed that "from fire, life sprang, and to ashes will life wither." Calderon shook his head. Many religious beliefs sprang from ignorance of things attributed to what happened naturally. The spell he was studying conjured fire that could be thrown or appear upon an object that was in your hand, such as a piece of wood. The passage said, Focus on your inner fire and project it outward onto where you want it. Those without discipline be warned: put forth too much energy, and you will be destroyed.

Calderon had never been able to master creating fire; most of the spells he knew were to do with making lights and conjuring electricity, such as what he had done to the strange dwarf. King Adam had once said, "Bangs and puffs of smoke are nice for show but fairly simple. Real skill comes from what you don't see yet affects the flow of the magic that exists around us."

Calderon seemed to always fall short, but he had learned all he could. He held out his hand, palm up, his fingers clenched like they were trying to squeeze an invisible ball. He concentrated on trying to focus, gathering the energy needed to make a flame. A small, thin stream of smoke rose from his hand . . . then nothing.

Cursing to himself in Dwarvish, Calderon took a deep breath and exhaled. "I'll never get the hang of fire. I mean, what the heck does the damn book mean 'call forth your inner fire.' Frustrated, Calderon firmly closed the dusty old book, put it back on the shelf he had gotten it from, then turned and left.

Outside the library, Calderon turned and made his way down the east hallway to the main hall. As he passed Bard's office, he saw light from under the closed door and heard shuffling papers. Best leave Bard to it, thought Calderon as he continued on to the main hall.

He entered the now-boisterous hall to find many of the inhabitants eating a stew of turnips, onions, and potatoes and drinking the strong dwarven ale they had received earlier in the week. In their usual spot in the corner, with a full bowl of soup in front of him and a tankard of ale, sat Kyle. His face and hands were covered with dirt. Calderon hurried over to him and sat down.

"So, what did they say?" asked Calderon with no preamble.

Kyle looked up from his dinner and grinned smugly. "It wasn't easy, you know. But Dad went and talked to Bard. When he came back, he had changed his mind and said I could go."

Calderon grinned widely. He was glad to know he wouldn't have to make the long journey alone.

"Are you coming to the fire? Some people said old Darm is going to tell a story," said Kyle.

Calderon looked at the windows perched high over the main hall doors. Through them, he could see the growing darkness. He nodded, accepting a bowl of stew and a tankard from the cook. Without warning, Molly sat down beside him with her own bowl of stew.

"I heard Darm is going to tell the tale of the Dragon's Tooth," said Molly.

"That's great,'" said Calderon, taking a bite of stew. Of all the stories that Darm told, the legend of the Dragon's Tooth was his favorite.

There had been many powerful weapons throughout time, but the Dragon's Tooth had belonged to the Kusarku kings. It was said to be able to cut through almost anything, and to be imbued with dragon fire. Long ago, the story went, a Kusarku had taken a tooth from an ancient dragon and made it into a weapon. It was even said that the holder could control dragons.

"I've heard that story a thousand times," complained Kyle.

There was a whomping sound from under the table, and Kyle made a face. Molly smiled, satisfied, and took another bite of soup. Calderon grinned at them. Those two often fought like family, and in fact, Kyle and Molly were cousins.

"So, how was your day, Molly?" asked Calderon.

Molly made a face. "Oh, the usual. Nothing new. She sighed. "Did you get the hang of that new sword of yours? It's so strange looking."

Calderon's face flushed. "I think I am starting to get it," he answered, taking a sip of his cool, refreshing ale.

"And what about you, potato head? Were you able to hit the target next to the one you were aiming for?" said Molly, giggling.

Kyle looked away and took a long drink from his ale to save him from answering.

"Not like you to be without words, or did you shoot an arrow over the wall?" joked Molly, and Calderon stifled a laugh.

"If you must know, I hit my target every time," said Kyle angrily.

Calderon cleared his throat, "Kyle and I are going to Alezadria," said Calderon, hoping to stop a fight and distract Molly.

"I know," she said sadly, worry lines appearing on her face. "It's all over the castle. Something about a weird dwarf."

Calderon nodded. "Two weird dwarves attacked me while I was out hunting, and Bard and I think they were on their way to attack Eldall. A human troll hunter who helped me is going to ask King Adam to gather the leaders of the races and tell about the attack so we won't have a war on our hands."

Kyle smiled. "And I'm going so Cal makes it back in one piece."

Calderon smiled in return.

"You two will be safe—right, Calderon?" said Molly, still worried.

"Of course," said Kyle, projecting a bit of arrogance with his voice and puffing out his skinny chest.

Calderon took a long draft of his ale and glanced through the windows to the growing darkness. Putting his empty tankard down on the table, he stood up and straightened his shirt.

"Well, shall we?" said Calderon.

He and his two friends left the great hall, heading toward a bonfire that was newly lit next to the base of the western wall.

Chapter 5

THE BONFIRE WARMED Calderon's face he sat with Kyle on his left and Molly on his right. The three friends, like everyone else in attendance, sat on small oak stools. Most of the castle's inhabitants were there. Everyone was silent, either looking at the fire before them or the night sky covered with its blanket of stars. Calderon looked up as well and was overcome with a sudden feeling he was like a miniscule speck in a vast amount of space. Beside him, he heard the repeated snick-snick sound of Kyle absent-mindedly whittling a small piece of cedar. Five people to Calderon's right sat Bard, and next to him, wrapped in a grey cloak sat Darm, hunched over. Darm and Bard both were staring deeply into the fire before them. Calderon looked toward it, too, and was soon lost in the flames, watching as small twigs curled up and burnt to ashes and larger branches caught. It was constant, never-ceasing, beautiful action.

There was a sudden loud pop as a large log burst, falling to the ashes below it and releasing a shower of sparks into the night sky like lightning bugs in the summer grass. Calderon looked around. Darm was now standing as straight and tall as his wizened frame would allow. Everyone's eyes were now on him. With his arms thrown out, palms up to the night sky, inviting everyone around him to participate, he began his tale in a strong, deep voice.

"Once, we were slaves. We looked more like farm animals than people. Once, we were nothing. We looked on as though we were mere peasants and farmers. Once, we were outlanders, uninvited people for whom there was no room in this world." Darm paused. Then, lowering his voice, he said, "And once, we were kings."

Calderon leaned forward. He loved hearing about how things once were.

Darm continued, "Listen, now, for this is how we gained and lost who we were.

"It began when our ancestors first came to this land from across the great Dark Woods. Our people found these mountains we now call home and tried their best to carve out a settlement. Our ancestors were beset by all manner of man and beast in the prospect of this goal. But worst of all were the dragons. Time and again, we would build our homes only to have the dragon fall upon us. And so it was that with the help of our greatest blacksmiths and sorcerers, the Dragon's Tooth was forged."

Calderon nodded to himself, remembering his history studies. He sometimes wondered if the Kusarku god Flagrash, The Great Flame, was actually attached to the Kusarkus' roots since living in the cold reaches of the Dark Woods meant fire was important. However, Calderon was not a believer in Flagrash. Fire was fire, a part of the natural way of things, and he didn't believe it needed some god to bring it into existence. Other Kusarkus were strong believers, especially nomads. They often burned themselves to be closer to their god.

Also, Calderon pondered, the Kusarkus had indeed been seen as outsiders and lesser people. One thing often forgotten was that the Gold Dwarves had been their allies. It made sense. Although they differed strongly in appearance, they both were similar in personality, being very stubborn, and with their love of metalworking. However, the dwarves at the time had been weakened by a long war between them and the Red Dwarves over some mine dispute. Calderon couldn't remember what was important about the mine, only that it was somewhere at the roots of the fire mountains. Also, the dragons had been a constant nuisance. So, the help the Gold Dwarves had been able to provide was sparse. Thus, the Kusarkus had to fend for themselves.

Darm continued, "The weapon took years to make. Many times, we failed, and many times we nearly gave up hope. In the end, under King Edward's direction, the blade was made. But only the king of the Kusarkus could wield the blade; all others were either consumed by the fire within it or nothing at all would happen. With the Dragon's Tooth, King Edward was able to protect against many enemies. The blade was without equal. It soon won the respect of the other races, and even the elves were soon our friends. It is said that the blade even staved off dragon attacks.

"Over the years, several attempts were made to steal the Dragon's Tooth for the other races feared the power the weapon held. Soon, its theft became inevitable, and the Dragon's Tooth was lost during the reign of King Brutus. With its loss, our race dwindled until our King Torin and Queen Elaine came to the throne. They brought our people together, and we were once again a race to be reckoned with.

In the fifth year of their rule, the Dark Elves arrived. They came from south of the Dark Woods in the southernmost region of the Seven Kingdoms. The Dark Elves were strong in magic and great in number; they soon laid siege to many of the strongholds of all the races. They made allies with some of the other races, like the goblins and trolls, and threw back even the armies of the elves. They were led by a cunning Dark Elf named Soren, who wielded a strange lance, which sucked the life from any it pierced. It was called the Shadow Lance.

"Seeing the seriousness of the situation, King Adam, the now human king who used to be high wizard, called a meeting. Torin and Adam put forth a plan to which the other races agreed: Torin would assemble his army at the foot of Stormbreaker Mountain. It was hoped that the threat of a large Kusarku army would push the Dark Elves to challenge our might. It was said that the Dwelling Elves helped spread the information, and the goblins passed it along to the Dark Elves as well. Soon, the Dark Elves took the bait.

"The Dark Elven army was massive—300,000 strong. Their feet shook the ground. Our own numbered barely 70,000, but our king stood strong. He knew he had to keep the Dark Elves distracted so the other races' armies could close in behind them. With King Torin in front of his army, he cried out, raising his weapon in challenge. Our ranks behind him raised their shields and roared as one with our king. We had little hope of surviving, but it did not matter. With the steep mountainside at our backs, we stood our ground.

"The enemy charged, with the goblins leading. Our shields met their charge. The enemy's first wave was thrown to the ground, and our spears came back bloody. Our king and his vanguard danced through the enemy ranks, cutting down everyone they met. The king left burning cinders in his wake. The Dark Elven army roared again, and more charged forward, heedless of those who had fallen, hoping to snuff us out in another charge. Spells cracked from the Dark Elves with lighting and fire. We could see the Dark Elves' king, Soren, on a black stallion, charging toward us from the rear, his long spear thrust forward.

"Then a cry emanated from above on the mountain behind us, and countless forms appeared on the mountainside. It was the elves, moving as one. Thousands of loosed arrows whistled through the air, landing and sometimes exploding in the ranks of the enemy. Not all the arrows met their mark, however. Some were knocked away by a gust of wind from the enemy spellcasters. From where the arrows did land, cries echoed in the valley as many fell and thrashed on the ground as the arrows pierced their flesh.

"The enemy—Dark Elves, goblins, and trolls—paused, raising shields above their heads and surveying the battlefield. Then they loosed the trolls from their chains within their ranks, and the trolls ran forward. With the enemy advance paused, there were bellows from the west mountainside, and a dwarven voice echoed in the valley as thousands more squat, burly forms appeared on the east and west mountainsides. The dwarves charged at the Dark Elves, and the Dark Elves turned to meet their advance.

"Just then, the elves on the mountain behind us fired another volley of arrows into the enemy's ranks. More screams of pain erupted from the enemy. Then a yell and a sickly green light came from the enemy's general. It was followed by a shriek from the mountain behind us. We turned to see many huge flying shapes descending on us and the elves. The elves turned and fired hurriedly. A few ran for cover. Many of the elves were engulfed in green and red flames as dragon-like creatures flew down on them.

"The dwarves charged into the enemy's ranks, but they were few in number. The enemy charged straight at us, yelling, with the trolls trampling all in their path. King Torin turned to us, no fear in his eyes. 'Today, this ends, and we make history. Know who we are,' he shouted. King Torin raised his sword high, and it blazed with an eager hunger. We charged forward, headless of the enemy's number. We had our brave king, and we would not be refused victory.

"We charged forward, meeting the enemy at the base of a small hill. It was deafening, the sound of steel on steel, steel on wood, steel cutting through flesh and bone. There were bangs of the spells being thrown about. Above it all, the hideous cries of people dying: Kusarku, dwarf, elf, troll, and Dark Elf. Though our king and our men cut down all in our path, we were too few. We were slowly losing ground, being pushed step by step back to the base of the mountain. A huge troll leapt at the ranks of our men, smashing shields and caving in helms. In the din, we heard our king: 'Fight on! Fight on! Push them back!' He leapt forward, and his sword seemed to flash as it cut the legs out from under the giant brute.

"Then a trumpet sounded, and many of the enemy glanced over their shoulders to where the noise had come from. At last, the humans and wizards had arrived. 'Hold the line!' yelled many voices from behind us. The enemy charged forward, trying to overwhelm one race at a time, most likely. However, the dwarves pushed them from each side and the wizards rained down spells upon them, forcing the enemy close together. All we had to do was hold out, and we would crush them. Suddenly, from within the line of enemy forces charged their leader, his lance lowered at our men, and a strange glow hung about the blade. He stabbed and cut his way through our forces. Whoever the blade touched began to wither before our eyes. His men charged into the hole their leader had made and cut down many behind our shield wall before racing back as our men ran forward.

"King Soren ran back to the top of the small hill. Our men were beginning to tire when the tide of the enemy let up. The human army had caught up, and from that direction, screams doubled. Our king ran again to the front. His armor dented and his helm gone, we could not tell if it was his blood or not that covered his armor. Still, he smiled as he charged forward, waving his sword over his head. 'For Dreadston!' he cried. He plowed forward through the enemy lines, and we stormed after him. What happened next few can explain. Most saw no further than their sword or spear in the chaos as all the armies crashed together. But when I reached the peak, I saw our king and Soren circling each other.

"The enemy leader lunged forward, and Torin dodged to one side. As he rolled to his feet, he swung out with his sword, catching it on the enemy's blade and pushed the long, sharp tip of the lance down into the dirt. Torin swung his leg up and kneed the enemy in the gut. In return, the enemy drew back, yanked his blade free of the ground, and swung the lance over his head in a circle, hitting Torin in the side of his face with the butt end of the weapon. Torin stumbled back, and the enemy charged forward, ready. Feet from him, Torin looked up, and with his left hand threw a spell that blasted the ground at the enemy leader's feet, throwing him backward. Torin straightened and threw his sword into the enemy's shoulder, where the blade seemed to burn into him. The enemy screamed as the blade buried itself in his right arm, and parts of the appendage began to turn black.

"As Torin reached him, the enemy lunged forward in desperation, stabbing with his remaining arm. Torin dodged, pulled his sword free, and brought his blade down through the shaft of the lance, splitting it in two. As the pole broke, there was an explosion of air that threw everyone back. As we all rose to our feet, an enormous, deformed creature flew out of the night and grabbed the enemy leader. Then there was a second explosion, and fireballs filled the night sky, falling only on the Dark Elves as they desperately tried to escape. When the fireballs stopped, on the peak of the small hill stood our King Torin, the now King Adam at his side. So ended the last battle of the Grey War.

"Our king was victorious, but the price was steep. As our group had been targeted most in the battle, we had lost much of our army. Things became worse when General Krasp led a failed coup that led to his exile."

At that moment, a large log in the middle of the fire broke and sent a burst of sparks into the night sky again. With that, Darm sat back down and wrapped his cloak tightly about him. The energy seemed to go out of him. He looked pale and sad as he gazed into the fire as if once again seeing the horrors of battle.

Calderon looked up into the star-laden sky, wondering. Beside him, Kyle did another stroke with his whittling knife. The shaving fell to the ground and blew away into the dark. Later, as Calderon walked back to his room and bed, he thought about the story he had heard and went over all the details. The fact that his father had been such a great warrior filled him with pride. However, he wondered why all old stories started with the Dragon's Tooth. It was funny how everything started there. Everything had a beginning and an end, a height and a fall.

Chapter 6

As Calderon lay in bed that night, he was still thinking about Darm's tale. He wondered what his parents had really been like. Could he ever measure up to them? And then, a much more important thought came to him: What would his parents think of their only son? His mind still a blur, he finally closed his eyes slowly and fell into a fitful sleep.

His confused dreams featured his parents coming in and out of focus. They changed like ripples on a lake interrupting each other and flowing over their bounds into one another. Suddenly, with bright clarity, he found himself on a green hill looking down on a familiar view, the human capital of Alezadria. He could hear birds and the murmur of travelers and merchants from where he stood. Calderon could also see guards, ever vigilant, moving back and forth on the great stone walls. A gust of wind blew Calderon's unbound hair, and he breathed deeply.

He jumped when someone cleared their throat behind him. He spun on his hooves, tearing up grass in his haste. There stood King Adam at his ease, his gnarled oak staff in his right hand. King Adam was tall with long white hair and a short white goatee. A scar ran above his right eye and up into his straight hair. His eyes were clear and bright blue, full of experience, but the set of his face was kindly and welcoming. King Adam smiled, walked up next to Calderon, and looked down on Alezadria.

Without looking at Calderon, King Adam said, "The world is in motion. It always is, and yet we are never in haste to hurry it along. However, we must force fate's hand and make a stand before the ground falls away beneath our feet." King Adam turned slightly and smiled warmly at Calderon. He put a large pale hand on Calderon's shoulder. "I'll be waiting for your arrival. Be safe during your travels."

As the dream faded away, Calderon looked down at his feet. There between them was a purple morning glory.

The dream changed. He was in a dark place; it was cold and as silent as the grave. He heard the distant drip of water onto damp cave floors. Calderon could feel the damp chill of the cave; it made him think of slimy things like salamanders. Shivering, he turned in his dream to survey the surroundings. With a start, he noticed an old, worn throne carved from the cave wall. At first, he thought the throne was empty, but with a second glance, he noticed a figure sat there in shadow, sprawled in an attitude that spoke of restlessness. As he watched the figure, it shifted and swore quietly.

"Enter, damn you. Stop skulking and plotting," said the figure in a high, crackling voice.

Calderon didn't move, afraid the rebuke was meant for him. Then came an unmistakable clip-clop of hooves. Calderon looked around, and there stood an immense figure, its huge horns swept back like a ram's. Red eyes flashed from the near darkness, and the sparse light glinted off a huge battle ax. The figure blew out a snort of hot air that steamed in the cave's bleakness.

With a start, Calderon awoke. Crackle stood over him and gently shook him. "Finally, you're awake, lad, by the Seven Kingdoms," said Crackle, exasperated. "Bard is waiting for you in his office." With an amused grunt, he turned and stomped out of the room.

Calderon flew from his bed and quickly dressed, his mind still buzzing with confusion from his dream. "Was it a dream, though?"" wondered Calderon aloud. He rumpled his long hair and then quickly tied it in a ponytail. Shaking his head, he grabbed his sword and put the cuff to his left wrist. He carefully wound the chain over his shoulder, feeling the cold links through his tunic.

Chapter 7

CALDERON HURRIED INTO the great hall, where several people were already breaking their fast. Lem and Crackle sat at a table in the corner, both drinking from large cups. Molly stood next to Darm, who was stabbing his eggs as though they personally had affronted him.

As Calderon crossed the hall, Molly hurried over to him. "Kyle is already in there with Bard, I think," said Molly with an anxious smile. From the kitchen came a horse yell of impatience from the cook, Sally.

"It'll be fine. You had better get your act together, or Sally will serve you for dinner," said Calderon teasingly.

Molly gave Calderon another look and a gentle squeeze on his arm before hurrying towards the kitchen. Calderon shook his head and smiled despite his own trepidation.

Calderon continued through the main hall, noting that Afred, who was short with pale skin and short black hair, and Don, tall and imposing, were on guard duty. Both were looking out through small arrow slits on either side of the door, watching something. Calderon wondered if it was anything important but didn't stop to ask. Soon, he was outside Bard's door. He knocked and opened the door to enter.

Bard sat with papers in front of him and a slight frown on his face.

Calderon cleared his throat and asked, "Anything wrong? Crackle said you wanted to see me."

Bard smiled smugly, "There is usually something wrong somewhere. What we need to focus on, though, is your travel to Alezadria."

Calderon smiled and nearly jumped for joy. "So, you got a letter from Adam?" he asked hopefully.

Bard nodded, holding up a scroll, which still gave off a hint of a magical charge. Calderon knew the message would have been delivered directly from King Adam to Bard by magical means. "Indeed. He says to come with all speed but also with caution. He sent a letter that will give you access to the city and castle." Bard seemed worried. His smile was gone, and his dark eyes glanced back down at the table.

"What is it?" asked Calderon, concerned.

Bard sighed. "It's a letter from the Gold Dwarves. Apparently, dwarves have been going missing of late, and they think trolls might have something to do with it, so there might be something to what Duncan said."

Calderon frowned too. It was strange for trolls to be anywhere in the area. "What are you going to do?"

Bard shrugged and answered sadly, "Not much we can do but increase our own watches and patrols. We don't have enough warriors to scour the whole of the Grey Mountains. But be that as it may, keep your own eyes open on your journey."

Calderon started as the large door flew open abruptly. In the doorway stood Kyle with a hefty pack on his shoulders, his bow, and a quiver full of arrows.

Bard laughed softly and thumped the table with his hand as if declaring something finished and rose to his hooves. Walking over to Calderon, he put an arm around his shoulder and handed him a scroll. Though he still smiled, his voice was stern. "Take this to the guards at Alezadria. The seal on it should gain you entry. And take care of each other. Our very fates could rest on you two succeeding in this mission. Be at this council that Adam has set up in five days." Bard gripped Calderon's shoulder tightly for a moment then he turned away and sat again behind his desk.

"Good luck and safe travels to both of you, and may your hooves never falter," said Bard gravely.

Calderon didn't know what to say. He was excited and nervous and sad all at once. In the end, he nodded, and with Kyle, he turned and hurried to his bedchamber to gather his bag.

An hour later, they were off with full packs and an earful of protest from Molly still in their ears. She was loath to be left behind. Both Kyle and Calderon were worried she would follow after them even though they both had sternly denied her wish to accompany them.

"It's not like she could keep up, anyway," said Kyle gruffly to Calderon as they walked past row after row of tilled fields. "She has no woodcraft. She's always been in the castle or on a farm."

Calderon nodded then, noticing Kyle wasn't looking at him, answered, "Yeah, and you heard Bard—we need to hurry. We want to make it to Alezadria in five days in time for this council."

They walked on in silence for a minute, then Kyle asked, "What was Bard so on edge for? I mean, besides this mission, he seemed like he had something on his mind. He went right back to looking at some papers as we left. I would have thought that he would have seen us off."

Calderon grinned at the way his friend was always so observant, and he told Kyle about the missing dwarves.

When Calderon finished, Kyle nodded. "Then Duncan wasn't lying. There really could be a troll around here." Kyle didn't look scared, though. In fact, he looked excited at the thought of a dangerous adventure.

Calderon grinned again. It was nice to be finally doing something, not just talking about what could be done. After a few minutes of silent trekking, he looked at Kyle and saw his eyes were fixed on the path in front of him.

"What's up? Did you eat something bad?" asked Calderon.

Kyle cleared his throat but kept his eyes pointedly forward. "The folks weren't happy about me leaving. They seemed to think the farm is where I belong," said Kyle. His face was expressionless, but his voice was full of sardonic fury. "They think that just because it's good enough for them to work on a farm that it should be good enough for me."

Calderon had often heard about the disagreements between Kyle and his parents. Kyle's parents had opposed Kyle learning even to shoot a bow. With a lighthearted voice to shake Kyle out of his mood, Calderon said, "Well, we are leaving now, and nothing can turn us around. We have a mission and a purpose from King Adam, and no one can argue that."

Kyle let out a long breath, and though he didn't say anything, his shoulders seemed to relax.

They continued following the path they had only days before been on when returning from Calderon's hunt near Eldall. Their goal was to reach Eldall, go around it to Aurum Lake, and then to travel along Pyrite River, which they could follow easily out of the mountains. After that, it would be only a few more days' journey to Alezadria. Calderon and Kyle hoped that by following the Pyrite River instead of an established trail, they could avoid dangers such as goblins or thieves that often waylaid travelers on the rough paths in the mountains.

The two talked at their ease and quickly covered mile after mile. Both Kyle and Calderon knew the woods of the Grey Mountains well, so the thick vegetation caused very little hinderance for them. Kyle was in front, his long arms good for moving low-hanging branches to prevent them getting caught in their horns.

"I came this way last summer and saw a cave bear eating the wild blueberries around here. We should pick some so we can eat as we walk," said Kyle nonchalantly. Calderon agreed heartily, and before long, they found blueberry bushes and began to pick the delicious fruit. Soon, their hands were sticky and stained purple.

Calderon laughed aloud. "This reminds me of the time we tried to make wine from the grapes that Darm had grown," he said.

Kyle laughed too. "But all we made was a mess with a little grape juice . . . and a pissed-off Darm. I thought he was going to skin us. I swear his face was as purple as the grapes," answered Kyle, trying but failing to stifle his laughter. The forest rang with their merry voices as they started off on their journey again.

When they finally reached the edge of Eldall, night had begun to fall around them.

"At last, we've made it," said Calderon with a sigh as he adjusted his pack on his shoulder to relieve some of the stiffness in his back.

Kyle swung his pack down and set his bow and quiver beside it. He then sprawled back into the thick mountain grass. Calderon followed suit, and the two lay looking up at the darkening sky as the stars began to glimmer. A half mile away, Eldall glowed even now with a warm light.

"How much longer till we get out of the mountains?" asked Kyle, who had never set foot outside the Grey Mountains.

Calderon yawned widely and answered, "At least another full day if we keep moving as we are."

"What do you think will happen when we get there? I mean, what is expected of us?" asked Kyle in a whisper.

Calderon thought he knew what would happen but thought it best to allay Kyle's fears. "We will represent the Kusarkus at this gathering. I will speak before those leaders who are assembled there, and King Adam will encourage the other races to make the right decisions. There are heroes and great people across the Seven Kingdoms who will rise to the summons of need," said Calderon in a voice he hoped was confident.

The two friends grew silent again, and in the quiet darkness, they heard many night creatures moving about their business. Wolves were gathering somewhere on a rocky mountainside to their right. Several owls could be heard staking claim to a hunting territory. And Calderon and Kyle were calmed by the familiar night sounds.

Then all became silent as if a spell had been cast. Calderon stiffened, listening with all his might. Then he heard something huge moving through the trees closer to Eldall but also in their direction. Together, Calderon and Kyle sprang to their hooves and as one, moved stealthily in the direction of whatever it was. Calderon's mind had gone blank. If he did have a thought, it was that whatever this was, it wasn't good.

On the edge of a clearing, the two waited. On the other side of it, a small stream ran babbling through the forest. When a massive creature emerged from the darkness, the two young Kusarkus held their breath. It was a troll. Calderon and Kyle had heard stories of trolls, but nothing had prepared them for the sight before them. It stood taller than a farmhouse, taller than the doors of Dreadston Castle—at least ten feet tall. Long, skinny arms hung to the troll's knees. It wore some sort of rough-looking animal skins. Small branches stuck in its wild hair, remnants of its lumbering trek through the forest. Although Calderon and Kyle couldn't see the troll's eyes, they knew they had to be small compared to the bulbous nose and enormous pointed ears that made up the creature's visage. And over the troll's huge shoulder was slung a large sack. As Calderon looked at it, a shiver went through his body. The sack moved and jerked as though something alive was inside it.

Chapter 8

Calderon and Kyle followed the troll as close as they were able without being discovered. Luckily, the troll never seemed to hear them, not even when Kyle tripped over a log or when Calderon rustled a shrub in passing. Soon, they reached a bend in the river. They were now just south of Eldall in the direction they had intended to travel. The troll, seeming comfortable, roughly threw down the bag. It landed with a thump and emitted a muffled cry of pain. The troll seemed unconcerned as it made its way to the water's edge and began cupping its hands to drink water.

Calderon and Kyle kneeled at the edge of the woods and began a hurried, hushed conversation.

"What do we do, Cal? Do we save whoever it is?" asked Kyle, sweat beading all over his forehead.

Calderon thought to himself, I can't just sit here and do nothing. I have to try and help. If I don't act now, I'll regret it later. Calderon wiped his own damp brow, scratched his chin, and nodded. "Why don't you distract it while I rescue whoever is trapped in that sack. Then we all run for it."

Kyle nodded determinedly and picked up a nearby rock. Taking careful aim, he threw the rock as far as he could into the river. The troll, not very smart, began to wade toward where the splash had happened, perhaps thinking it was a fish jumping.

Calderon hurried from his hiding place and drew his sword, which slid silently from its scabbard. He quickly slashed the top off the bag and concentrated hard on his magic. He imagined a hand covering the captive's mouth to cover any noises he or she might make, then he released his spell. A short figure hooded in green began to struggle to free itself from the bag while making frantic, muffled cries of distress. Calderon sheathed his sword as he leaned down to whisper, "We are here to help you. Can you run?"

The figure paused its struggle and turned in Calderon's direction. Calderon was aware of shrewd eyes taking him in; then the figure nodded.

Calderon grabbed hold of the being under an arm and pulled the figure to their feet. Whoever they were, they must obviously be a dwarf for they barely stood over four feet tall. The two turned and began to run to where Kyle stood waving at the forest's edge. They were nearly to the dense cover of trees when, looking up, Calderon saw Kyle's eyes widen. That was his only cue as he grabbed the dwarf and leapt forward. Wind whistled by his right ear, and a huge river stone crashed into the forest ahead of him with a large crunch.

Calderon looked around as the troll roared, reaching for another stone to crush them into jelly.

"Run for it!" yelled Calderon. Kyle and Calderon each grabbed the dwarf under an arm, and the three took off as a second stone followed the first. Calderon concentrated hard and sent a ball of electricity over his shoulder as he ran. The troll howled again, this time in pain.

"Nice one," yelled Kyle as the three pushed through bushes and low-hanging limbs, heedless of the branches whipping their faces and arms.

They ran for at least an hour, and the sounds of the angry troll had long ceased when the three reached a clearing. They all fell to the ground, breathing hard. Calderon was covered in sweat and had small cuts all over his face. He was sure his companions were in no better shape than he was. Then suddenly, all three began to laugh, and for a while, they couldn't stop.

Calderon finally sat up and looked around. They were still near the

Pyrite River; he could hear it babbling off to his right. The dwarf stood up and lowered his hood. However, it wasn't a he; it was a she!

Kyle stood up too. "What in the Seven Kingdoms are you doing out here?"

The female dwarf scoffed, "As if a girl dwarf can't herself leave the kitchen or her sewing. Oh, please. I may be a girl, but I can usually take care of myself."

Kyle blushed deeply, and Calderon cleared his throat.

"Even if a woman should be out and about," Calderon said, "how did that troll get ahold of you?"

The dwarf glanced at him. "My name is Sara, and I was doing a geologic survey," she said with a tone of importance.

Calderon stood up and moved closer to Sara. She looked to be a dwarf about their own age. Her hair was blond like that of most Gold Dwarves, but it was long and tied in a braid that fell to her slim waist. She had bright green eyes and a pretty face, though at the moment, it was scowling. Calderon hoped Kyle wouldn't ask where her beard was.

"But what would a surveyor be doing in order to get caught by a troll? And wouldn't you have guards or something?" asked Calderon.

Kyle nodded, hoping his earlier comments would be forgotten.

Sara's gaze dropped to her well-worn leather boots, and she began to chew on her lip, obviously thinking. Calderon couldn't help but notice her full, supple lips. She was really pretty, and he hoped he wouldn't blush at that thought. Then Sara stamped her foot and sat down with a huff.

"Seeing as you saved me, I might as well be honest. We are dealing with a problem: the gold veins we usually mine are pretty well tapped, and we need to keep up with the demand. So, surveyors have been going out to find new places to mine. My father was one of them." Sara's expression held sadness at the mention of her father, and Calderon thought he saw her eyes were over-bright as he and Kyle sat down near her.

Kyle was haphazardly dabbing at a cut above his eye with a spare cloth. Sara sighed, and as Calderon passed her a water skin, Sara gratefully took a drink and continued.

"People have been disappearing right and left when they leave Eldall, but ol' Dad thought he had found a likely spot and went to look into it. He said there was plenty of pyrite, galena, and quartz about, and you know what that means." Calderon nodded, but Kyle shrugged. Sara grunted, "It means, goat boy, that there is very likely gold around too."

Calderon smiled and looked at Kyle, who was staring at a tree and grinding his teeth.

"Anyway, dear ol' Dad never came back. So, I went out to look for what he had talked about. I had to go; everyone was looking everywhere other than there," added Sara, her slightly chubby cheeks flaring with passion. After a moment, she said, "Anyway, you can guess the rest. I snuck out, and before I knew it, I was in a stinky ol' sack. But who are you two?"

Kyle cleared his throat importantly. "Well, I'm Kyle, and this is Calderon, and we are on an important mission to see King Adam."

Calderon could have stamped on Kyle's hoof; he didn't have to tell everyone what was going on. What if word got out and someone tried to prevent them from getting to the council?

At that moment, Sara's eyes grew as large as dinner plates. She dove forward, tackling both Kyle and Calderon to the ground. Then a tree trunk flew through the air and landed where they had just been only seconds before. Calderon blinked in surprise. Sara screamed as a gargantuan hand grabbed her and lifted her into the air. Kyle and Calderon rolled to their feet to face the challenge before them. It was the troll again, with Sara hanging from one huge hand, her feet kicking wildly.

With astounding speed, the troll swung its other enormous arm around to smack Kyle. Kyle barely dodged out of the way. Calderon gritted his teeth and drew his sword. The troll turned and made his lumbering way towards the forest's edge.

Calderon glanced at Kyle and yelled, "We can't let him get away!"

Kyle's bow was already in hand, and with one fluid motion, he drew an arrow, set it to the string, and fired. The arrow flew like an angry hornet and buried itself in the troll's right shoulder. The troll stopped and roared in anger, half turning towards them. Calderon, without pausing to think, threw his sword. The strong chain wrapped around the troll's left leg about the knee, and the blade cut deep into the flesh. The crossguard acted like a brace, holding the chain in place.

Running at full speed, Calderon moved past the troll and pulled as hard as he could, digging his hooves deeply into the hard earth, causing the troll to topple over onto its side. Calderon swiftly moved back towards the fallen creature to help Sara, who was struggling free of the troll's suddenly loose grip. As Calderon ran, he swung the chain in a circle, unwinding it from the troll's leg. Then, with a jerk, he pulled the sword free. The troll roared in pain and made a wild grab at Sara just as Calderon reached her.

To Calderon, everything seemed to slow down; he saw the huge hand coming at them, grasping. Calderon wondered if his sword would cut through the troll's thick, strong fingers. But he saw the fear on Sara's face and felt his resolve harden. He willed his blade to slash through the troll's fingers. Then, in a flash of red, Calderon sliced off three of the troll's immense digits. The troll roared in pain and rolled away from them.

Calderon and Sara ran together toward Kyle as the troll's roars turned into a scream of fury. Kyle stood at the edge of the forest, one arrow notched and drawn back. There was another bellow from the troll, and Kyle fired. The creature again let out a scream—this time, one of pain. Calderon reached Kyle's side and looked back. Though the troll was missing its fingers, there was very little blood, much less than there should have been. The finger stubs appeared black. He also saw Kyle's arrow stuck fast in the troll's left eye, while its remaining eye was full of hate and fury as it glared at its escaping prey.

Turning his back on the troll, Calderon ran into the forest after his friends. He knew they had to keep moving and get away.

We've wounded it, but I don't think we stand a chance in a straight fight. We have to keep running. But we need to stay close to the river so we don't lose our way, thought Calderon. Then he took the lead, yelling, "This way! Follow me."

When the trio finally stopped, Calderon was exhausted and sore all over. Daylight was just peeking between the trees, and the coos of mourning doves could be heard along with the rustling of pheasants.

"We should be safe for now with daylight here," said Sara with a yawn.

Kyle pointed out a thicket to rest in, and he and Sara both lay down on their backs after removing their gear and fell asleep. Calderon, too, lay down but stared up at the dense canopy. It had been a crazy night with so much to consider. Should he bring Sara along? And should he tell her everything?

Thinking back, he realized she had saved his and Kyle's lives. That tree trunk could have at least seriously hurt if not killed them. Then where would they have been? Bard was depending on him. With these thoughts swirling in his head, he fell asleep.

Calderon awoke to the sounds of chewing. It was Kyle noisily eating an apple as Sara yawned and stretched, her blond braid disheveled. Calderon knew he couldn't look much better than the others. He cleared his throat, and Kyle tossed him a water skin. Taking a draft to wet his throat, he asked, "How are we all?"

Kyle grinned. "Just peachy. Always wanted to play hide and seek with a troll."

Sara grinned, too, and agreed, saying, "I'm alive and pretty well owe ya. So, why don't you fill me in on what's going on? I certainly don't have anything holding me back from leaving Eldall now that ol' Dad is gone. But I gotta keep moving and doing the best I can."

Calderon stood up and stretched. As he gathered up his things, Calderon considered what and how much to tell Sara, if anything at all. However, for some reason, things felt different now. They had saved each other, and some sort of makeshift trust had been established between them. Plus, she was a dwarf; it wasn't like she was an elf.

Calderon turned to face Kyle and Sara. "As Kyle said, we are on our way to Alezadria. I'll tell you the story as we walk," offered Calderon, making eye contact with Sara, who nodded and began patting down the wrinkles in her traveling hood. Kyle stood up, too, and gathered his things with some small groans of protest as he put his pack on his shoulders. Then the three turned and headed in the direction of the Pyrite River to continue on their journey.

Chapter 9

Calderon's hooves were already hurting from the rough, unforgiving mountain rocks. However, he made no comment on it. Instead, he continued telling Sara his tale.

Sara walked in front. She seemed to know the mountains well. During Calderon's story, she asked many questions: How well did Calderon know Alezadria? How did he know it so well? He soon found himself telling her what felt like his life's history.

In turn, Sara seemed very smart and picked up on the implications of the strange dwarves as well as the unusual glowing ball they had come across.

However, she didn't seem to care much for what the elves thought about things. Indeed, as with most dwarves, she viewed most elves with contempt. "Who cares what they think? They think and talk too much when they could be doing things," Sara had said scornfully.

As they continued on, Calderon tried to get to know Sara better, as did Kyle. While they talked, Calderon walked a few feet away, holding the sword on its chain and swinging it in little circles. He was still amazed by how light the blade was. With the slightest pressure on the chain, he could change the direction of the blade. As he swung it faster, he tried making figure eights, soon increasing his speed and with less concern that the blade would hit him.

Kyle seemed much less tense than he had at first, and indeed, he seemed to enjoy Sara's company. This did surprise Calderon. Kyle had always found it easy to make new friends . . . except when it was a girl.

Kyle walked along, a little behind Sara, surreptitiously polishing his horns.

"Have you ever been outside of the mountains?" Sara asked Kyle.

Kyle shook his head. "Naw, Mom and Dad always needed me, and there was never a reason for me to go anywhere else."

Sara smiled. "I used to sneak out to go see the land around the mountains. It's so flat and open. I think it's exciting to actually be going down there."

Calderon put in, "My first time was scary. I felt like there was nowhere to hide, like being a mouse watched by a great owl. There are so many people of so many different races in Alezadria. It was a little intimidating, so I only stayed in the castle, at first."

They had walked throughout the day and indeed were now nearing the edge of the mountains and could get their first good look at the land below.

Kyle and Sara saw an opening in the forest before them and hurried forward into the quickly approaching evening light. Calderon smiled and followed more slowly. When he reached the other two, he stopped as well and looked down on the land opening up below them. To their right, the Pyrite River shot over a cliff into a waterfall, sending up sprays of water that made many small rainbows in the soft light. The Pyrite River then snaked its way south until it joined with several other mountain rivers, such as the White River and the Boring River to form Elizdiath Lake, which sat to the south of the great elven capital, Elizdiath.

Directly below them on small rolling hills was a great expanse of farmland. It was said that most of the agriculture in the Seven Kingdoms came from the farms that were between them and Alezadria to the southwest. The farmland also ran directly west to the Snake River that came down from the Red Mountains at the other side of the country. On the far side of Elizdiath Lake were the Great Plains and beyond them the Dark Woods, which were said to go on forever as no one had seen their entirety. There, the Wood Elves lived, but they didn't say if they knew what was beyond the woods.

Looking southeast, Calderon imagined seeing a deep green shadow he knew was the Fairy Woods. There were dark tales of those woods. Magic and legend ran wild there. Though the Fairy Woods were not a large area, people who walked into them often didn't come out again.

Calderon glanced over at his friends to see their reaction. Kyle stood with his mouth agape, while Sara looked below her, her green eyes glinting with the excitement of adventure. Calderon laughed, and the other two looked at him.

"It looks like these hills and farms go on forever," said Kyle, awestruck, and Sara nodded her agreement.

Calderon pointed and said, "If we follow the Pyrite River to where it bends there—slightly to the southeast—we will come upon the main road. It is supposed to run from Elizdiath to Alezadria and even on to Harlech, where the Snake River comes down from the Red Mountains."

Sara nodded. "I had heard that the Red Dwarves use the Snake River to send their shipments out of the Red Mountains to Harlech and thence across the land to their destination."

"How do you know so much if you have never seen it?" asked Kyle.

"Because we give them the gold and other minerals they fashion into things. We, of course, want to be paid. So, we have to know where our supply is going. It's our livelihood! I mean, as you told me, Calderon, would Bard send out his supply without knowing where it was going?" Sara asked.

Calderon answered evenly, "That is part of the reason Bard wanted me to see the world outside of the mountains, I think."

"Well, I understand the part about a road and such, but how do we get down there? This is a cliff, after all, and that is a waterfall. How do people usually get down?" asked Kyle, scratching the base of his horns.

Sara sighed and shook her head, causing her blond braid to swing hypnotically, and looked away.

Calderon, however, pointed and answered, "Next to the falls is a merchant path that snakes down the cliff's side."

Kyle nodded, and the three walked over to the path. But Calderon thought he heard Kyle mutter, "We are still high up, though." Calderon shook his head; he knew Kyle hated heights.

When they reached the path, they found it was in good repair. It was cut into the cliffside itself, and instead of being made of dirt, it was formed of rock. Calderon's hooves, being used to mountain rock, found easy purchase. He thought as he walked, Could this be why some people make jokes about the Kusarkus being related to mountain goats?

Sara, as if trying to make a point, walked next to Calderon but close to the edge, nonchalantly looking down over it. Kyle, on the other hand, took up the rear, for once, and slid along with his back pressed against the wall.

After a few minutes, Sara said loudly back at Kyle, "We'd better hurry; I heard rocks sometimes break away here because of how loud the falls are."

Kyle turned pale but kept his position along the wall and walked as if he were on a tightrope.

When Sara and Calderon got to the bottom, they sat down in the thick, soft grass next to the river and watched Kyle on his way down. Every now and then, Calderon or Sara would yell something like "You're halfway down. Look how far you have come!" or "Look, Kyle—there's a turtle gaining on you."

When Kyle finally reached the bottom, he was pale and shaking. Calderon walked over to him and handed him his water skin, which he had filled from the quickly running water. Kyle drank eagerly but refused for a while to look at his companions. Instead, he started counting his arrows.

"Any better?" asked Sara soberly after a few minutes.

Kyle nodded. "It wasn't that bad. Plus, we are done with that now."

Calderon chose not to point out that when returning to Dreadston, they would have to go back up the path. He figured it was better to talk about that later.

"The first time I came out of the mountains, I felt naked and on stage for all to see. I wanted to flee and hide. You guys will be okay, though.

Just follow my lead. I know where to go," said Calderon, adding quietly to himself, "At least I think I do." He also hoped they wouldn't run into too many elves on the main road.

Sara jumped to her feet. "What are we waiting for—winter wolves to come? Let's go." With that, she took off towards the road like a shot.

Calderon followed her, and after a deep breath, Kyle followed as well, looking back over his shoulder, as had Calderon. Calderon noticed Sara didn't look back, though. Despite Sara moving her short legs at a very quick pace, Calderon and Kyle soon caught up to her. Sara's smile was huge, and her eyes were full of wanderlust.

When they reached the main road out of breath from their sprint, they looked in each direction. They couldn't see anyone traveling, but that was unsurprising this far from any town. They had around thirty miles to cover to get to Alezadria.

"I was expecting a bit more from the main road of the Seven Kingdoms," bemoaned Kyle, looking down at his mud-covered hooves with distaste.

Sara nodded her agreement. "As many supplies as are sent across the country, I would have thought smooth roads would make things easier. I mean, think of all the wheels and axles that are broken by rough roads."

Calderon looked down at the road surface; it was indeed travel-worn. Hoping to cheer his companions, Calderon offered, "The roads are mostly paved with stone as you get closer to cities. Think about it, Sara: you will soon see the walls of Alezadria made by Landon the Dwarf King. And, Kyle, you will be able to see your Archers' Guild at work. I often see the archers posted on the wall instead of foot soldiers."

With a skip forward, Sara started off. Calderon guessed she needed no more convincing.

"If we do see people on the road, just don't draw attention to yourself. Remember there are many Kusarkus roaming the lands," said Calderon as he walked beside Kyle.

Kyle curled an eyebrow. "So, we don't try to hide anymore or try wearing hoods or something?" asked Kyle.

Calderon answered confidently, "Those who try to hide themselves often just cause people to look at them harder. We are just one more group of travelers on the road."

"And anyway, how would you wear a hood, Kyle?" asked Sara, teasing.

Kyle blushed, and Calderon heard him mutter under his breath. Sara walked along with a spring in her step. Calderon wondered if she was always so confident or if it was an act. Kyle then seemed to think of something and quickened his step until he walked next to Sara. Calderon watched with an amused smile.

Kyle pulled out his hunting knife and proffered it to Sara. "You shouldn't be the only one without a weapon," said Kyle. Even from behind, Calderon could see the flush of Kyle's embarrassment.

Sara took the knife and hefted its weight. "It's a good knife. Thank you. I will remember this," responded Sara, gently touching Kyle on the elbow.

Calderon smiled. Kyle had always been shy around women when there had been an opportunity for him to run into them, which was a rare occasion. Calderon cleared his throat and skip-stepped to catch up.

"Since we have time, why don't we keep going a couple more hours and then turn in early? We can have a good dinner and rest. Then, tomorrow, if we get up with the sun, we can reach Alezadria by noon on the next day," said Calderon.

Kyle nodded. "I've seen a lot of rabbits around. I could cook some up for dinner."

When they finally found a place to camp under two huge oak trees not far from the road, Kyle went off into the tall grass that ran along both sides of the roadway. Sara and Calderon set about gathering fallen wood and brush to build a fire, but Calderon and fire never seemed to mix, so he was worried about trying to build one and looking foolish in front of both Kyle and Sara. Surreptitiously, he glanced at Sara, who was bent over the pile of wood. He couldn't see what she was doing, but soon, he saw the merry glow of a fire. Calderon sighed in relief as he walked over and sat next to her. She was gazing into the growing flames, every now and then adding a larger stick until the fire was large enough to stay lit on its own.

"You seem to know your way around a campfire," said Calderon.

Sara nodded, for once not showing off her big smile. "Me and ol' Dad made a lot of camps. He always wanted to be out and about and never wanted to be at home. He always said, 'If you stop moving and thinking, you stop doing.' I learned a lot from him about rocks and camping but not much else." She looked at Calderon with a wan smile then said, "Having the chance to go outside the mountains, and having you and Kyle with me, is a dream come true. I always felt like the world was too small—do you know what I mean?"

Calderon nodded. "Trust me; I know exactly what you mean. This whole thing of going to Alezadria got started when I couldn't stand to stay shut up in Dreadston anymore. The world does seem small when everything is familiar."

Then there was a crunch of gravel behind them, and they both turned at the sound, worried it was trouble. Calderon conjured a small floating light to appear at the edge of the camp. However, it was only Kyle, his horns giving him away even in the twilight.

He had a brace of rabbits already skinned, and he was grinning wildly with pride. "They were pretty easy to catch," said Kyle. He sat down and began attaching the rabbits to strong sticks he could use to turn the meat as it roasted over the fire.

As the rabbits cooked, Calderon stared up at the sky, watching as stars slowly came out. The moon was nearly full and gave good light to see by. Sara sat spinning Kyle's knife in her left hand, getting used to its weight.

Suddenly, Kyle said, "Why do you send everything you mine to the Red Dwarves? Why don't the Gold Dwarves smith their own materials like we do?"

Calderon realized he had never thought about the why of that and looked to Sara as well. The Red Dwarves had always been the smiths; it was just what was done, as far as he knew.

Sara lifted her eyebrows at them. "You two don't know?"

Calderon and Kyle shook their heads in response, and Calderon leaned closer to Sara, hoping to learn something new and maybe useful.

"One reason we don't smith what we mine is because of the amount that we mine. Do you know how much fire and labor it would take to smith that much material? We put most of our people into mining, so few are left to smith along with meeting the other requirements of living in the mountains."

Calderon shrugged. "I didn't know there were more Red Dwarves than Gold Dwarves."

Sara nodded. "Unlike us, the Red Dwarves have more than a dozen cities. We have only three."

Kyle turned the rabbits over and asked, "Okay, numbers make sense, but what was this about the amount of fire that could be produced?"

Again, Sara looked from one to the other, visibly astonished that they didn't know something. Then she went on in a tone as if teaching children. "We all know that the Fire Mountains in the north are attached to the Red Mountains. Well, the lava veins that are in the Fire Mountains are in the Red Mountains as well. Apparently, the Red Dwarves create fissures and tunnels toward these veins. The heat from the lava flows upward through pipes into a series of smithies that use the constant heat to do their work."

Kyle looked astonished. "Don't the Fire Mountains erupt, though? What if a vein or whatever erupted?"

Sara laughed. "Even if it did happen, the Red Dwarves would say it was worth the risk."

Calderon compressed his lips. It made sense, but it did sound like they were playing with fire.

Kyle, however, looked starry-eyed. "That sounds amazing! I hope I can see it one day."

Sara nodded. "Me too. I've only heard about what it looks like and how it works, but seeing it would be so different."

"Let's take things one step at a time," said Calderon, hating to be the person to bring them back to ground. "We still have to get to Alezadria first."

Kyle sighed, removed the rabbits from the fire, and set them on a flat rock to cool. Calderon moved forward to start cutting the meat into pieces for each of them.

However, Sara rushed forward eagerly. "Time to test out this knife."

In a matter of moments, the rabbits were cut into nicely sized pieces, and Sara turned to them and said with a grin, "Dinner is served. Obsidian sure is sharp," added Sara, staring lovingly at her new knife.

Once they had eaten their fill, the three laid down around the hot coals to sleep.

Calderon found himself running his right hand over the cuff that was attached to him. It felt old and worn and cold to the touch though it had been on him all day. He wondered at his weapon again; he had never seen or heard of a weapon like it. He wished he knew if he was using it right. If only his father were around to ask him. His father had won a great battle with the very same weapon attached to his wrist. Calderon thought back to fighting the troll. The way he had used it then was almost unconscious, as though the weapon had followed his will more than his movements. If anyone could help him learn more, it was King Adam. He always gave good advice. With those comforting thoughts, Calderon closed his eyes.

It was Sara who woke first in the morning. She stood above Calderon, stretching, her blond hair undone from her braid and cascading to the small of her back. The way it caught the morning light, it looked as if it were spun gold.

After a moment, Sara noticed Calderon was awake, too, and gazing at her. She smiled at him.

"Good morning. How much longer will it take to get there?" asked Sara.

Calderon heard Kyle wake up and stretch then answered, "We will travel all day today but get to the city by tomorrow. Why do you ask?"

She laughed and answered happily, "I'm just excited to see Alezadria. I've heard so much about the walls that I can't wait to see them." Then she turned and wished Kyle a good morning.

Kyle looked weary, his horns covered in dirt, probably from him moving in his sleep. As he sat up, he self-consciously began cleaning them as Calderon turned to get his pack ready to travel.

Within a few minutes, the three travelers were on the road again.

The farms that had been around them on all sides had given way to small, wooded areas polka-dotted across the land, creating havens for the wildlife that would move from one to another. They weren't like forests that covered the mountains; those had been overgrown and, for the most part, untamed.

Kyle asked as they walked, "What type of animals could live in such small areas?"

Calderon grinned, knowing the hunter that Kyle was, and said, "Mostly deer and smaller animals, but I've heard that farmers have a hard time with roaming groups of wolves and wild dogs."

Kyle frowned. "How could a pack of wolves hide with so little area for cover?"

Calderon shrugged. "For one thing, their hunting skills probably aren't as good as yours. But seriously, I'm sure any wolves could find ways to hide. Nature always finds a way."

Kyle smiled at Calderon's compliment and looked at the nearest group of trees with curiosity.

"Ohhhh no, mister. We are getting to that city soon, not in a week," said Sara, nudging him along. Kyle laughed and kept walking, but Calderon caught him giving the woods a last look as they went along.

As they got closer mile by mile to Alezadria, the road became more and more busy. They saw many different races, although humans comprised the vast majority. There were High Elves, Dwelling Elves, Gold and Red Dwarves, a few Kusarkus, and even a pair of Sobek pulling a hand cart laden with knitted rugs. Calderon caught Kyle and Sara looking at the Sobek with interest; it was clear they had never seen one. The Sobek, as a race, were tall and skinny with the slender body of a runner or swimmer and with long, clever fingers. Their heads were shaped like that of a crocodile, and they had the eyes of a predator. They lived along the rivers throughout most of the valley lands and down to the ocean that lay in the southwest.

Calderon was glad he had spoken to his friends before they had reached the busier areas of the road. He had set them each with a sharp glance, saying, "Remember: don't draw attention to yourself. We are just three more travelers on the road. Mind your own business and don't show off your weapons."

Kyle gave Calderon a penetrating stare in response. "That goes for you as well, Cal."

Calderon blushed deeply and turned away to walk on. He had developed a habit of switching his weapon around in its small circles and figure eights so much that he had begun to develop a callus on his palm.

Chapter 10

"WHERE ARE WE stopping for the night? Any chance of some good food and beer?" asked Kyle hopefully as he noisily crunched an apple.

"Yeah! I could go for a bed after that night I had with the troll. And last night, I swear to you, a tree root was growing beneath me," said Sara, rubbing the small of her back.

Calderon rolled his eyes exaggeratedly. He was nervous already about the coming council. Every footstep closer to Alezadria seemed to make things worse. Therefore, he wasn't exactly wanting to hurry along. I feel like I'm walking into a trap, thought Calderon. But there were a few towns between where they were and Alezadria, and if he was being honest with himself, a fresh, hot meal and a nice, cozy bed did sound good to him.

"There is a town on our way; it's called Crescent. I went through it the last time I was in the valley lands," Calderon said. "They have a bar there called Gallagher's. I've heard that they have some of the best food and beer around Alezadria."

Sara lifted an eyebrow at Calderon, saying, "Oh, and who is your source? I can't help but notice you always seem to know someone who knows something." She giggled as Calderon blushed and Kyle chuckled to himself.

"One of the people who trained me is Sir Kon. He is head of the guards in Alezadria. He told me about a lot of places where I could find good food and drinks when traveling. I suppose he was right to tell me about it because now it's coming in handy." Then, feeling as though he had to explain himself, he added, "I don't know everything or everyone. It's just that the people who trained me wanted me to be well informed." Calderon felt like a precocious child trying to defend his actions. Both Kyle and Sara were grinning and snickering at each other.

Calderon blew out an impatient breath. "So, do you two idiots want my suggestion or not?" asked Calderon with mock anger.

Kyle put up his hands. "Of course. We're in. You had me at good food."

Calderon looked away and grinned to himself. Sara started to whistle a tune as she walked at her ease, as if now she were on a morning stroll . . . which Calderon guessed they were, in a way.

As they walked, the trees became more numerous, the prairie giving way to a well-tended wooded area. The path snaked its way through the trees with the smell of sweet gum thick around them. The trees arched over the path like a ceiling of branches, making for a pleasant walk. Squirrels ran hither and thither. A bird twittered somewhere nearby, and then the woods were full of the sound of songbirds. A bit further on, a woodpecker's rhythmic knocking echoed through the foliage.

The three companions turned a bend in the road and saw the small village. It had no gates guarding it and no walls, either.

"How do they defend themselves?" asked Kyle.

Calderon laughed, looking at the small wood-and-brick building. "I don't think they worry about an army trying to besiege their nonexistent towers. And even if someone tried to rob or attack these people, I'm sure the residents know these woods better than anyone. Just think of how the Wood Elves use that concept, and you'll know what I mean."

Sara nodded and teased Kyle, saying, "Not all the world is doom and gloom. There are normal people here too."

Kyle rolled his eyes. "I know that," he said with a little embarrassment.

With the suddenness of a lightning bolt, all went quiet. They all looked around, slowing their walk and moving closer together. Calderon scratched the scar on his chin nervously. Then, with a whoosh of feathers, a red-shouldered hawk flew over them to land in a nearby tree.

They all laughed, and Calderon put an arm around each of his friends as they relaxed. The hawk shuffled and stared at their backs with an inscrutable yellow eye as they made their way into the small town of Crescent. Then, with a satisfied cry, the hawk flew off to its business—to report its findings.

They looked around as they entered Crescent. The houses were not squashed together as in big cities, and they were made out of a wide variety of materials. Most were small but looked comfortable. Their inhabitants moved about the town in the slow, relaxed manner of country folk with nothing pressing them to act like anything but themselves. From somewhere came the laughter of children, who next ran into the street, still laughing, chasing a dog that carried a large stick in its mouth.

Some of the villagers watched Calderon and his friends pass with a curious stare then went back to whatever they had been doing. The streets of the town were not paved. They were just hard-packed dirt from all the feet that had walked upon them. Calderon smiled at the people he saw. It made him happy to see people living their lives just as they always had and, Calderon hoped, always would.

The inn, Gallagher's, was easily the largest building of the town. It had two floors and was made of logs expertly set in place. The large open door was a welcome sight to footsore travelers. From inside came the friendly sounds of singing and laughter.

Kyle slapped Calderon's back, saying, "You know, for the first time during this journey, I'm looking forward to one of your ideas."

They all laughed and stepped inside.

Calderon looked around the room and scratched his chin. The room was populated mostly by humans, probably inhabitants of the town. However, there were a few dwarves, with long red beards, sitting by the fire. They were drinking from tall tankards. Next to the stairway leading to the bed chambers was a table of three Kusarkus. They leaned close together, talking in hushed voices. The tables, including the bar, were made of some kind of dark wood. Behind the bar, wiping out a glass, was an older human.

Kyle led the way to the bar, followed by Sara and Calderon. Calderon watched the other patrons, especially the deserter Kusarkus. For the most part, the humans ignored them or just gave them a bored glance. Then one of the Kusarkus at the table raised a dark-skinned hand. Calderon returned the greeting. Even if the others were traitors, it wouldn't be good to snub them and bring unwanted attention to Calderon's group.

Kyle slapped a hand on the bar and confidently asked the bartender, "What's good here, barkeep?"

The elderly human, wrinkled skin hanging on his bony frame, gave him a raised eyebrow. Sara elbowed Kyle, saying, "Sorry about my friend. What he means is we could use a drink, a hot meal, and beds for three, if you have them. The road out there has been rough."

Calderon did his best to hide his grin. It had been very fortunate that they had met Sara.

The barkeep smiled and gestured at an empty table a few feet away from the other Kusarkus. "The roads are definitely getting rough. Take a seat right over there. I'll be right over," he said in a pleasant voice. He was tall with short white hair and a neatly trimmed beard. His bright blue eyes, which seemed to inspect the three travelers, looked out through round wire glasses.

Calderon and his friends went to the table and sat down. Kyle groaned with relief and rubbed at one of his hooves. Then he surreptitiously straightened his tunic and touched both horns as though making sure they were still there. Calderon smiled to himself. Kyle always worried about how he looked and never wanted to appear like, as he said it, "A dumb, hick farmer and nothing else." Sara, too, was straightening out her braid as she gazed interestedly at the red-bearded dwarves. Calderon wondered how he himself looked and quickly tied up his hair with the plain leather cord he always carried.

The barkeep soon walked over to them, drying his hands as he came. Calderon saw he had long but strong-looking fingers. "What can I get ya?" he asked kindly.

Calderon cleared his throat, and the barkeep gave Calderon the full weight of his bright, inquisitive eyes. "A friend of mine, Sir Kon, said I could find good food and drink here. My friends and I are on our way to see him."

The barkeep's eyes sparkled with a friendly air. Then he threw back his head and laughed. It was a full, hearty sound, as though the old man poured everything into it. "How is the bull? Has he found a drink he can't finish?" he asked, shaking with his laughter.

Calderon laughed, too, and answered, "No, nor clothes that can fit him." Calderon's friends smiled hopefully like people did when they were trying to get in on a joke.

"Well, any friend of Sir Kon's is a friend of mine. Call me Gene," said the barkeep. "And as for food, I think I know what that giant meant. Give me a minute, and I'll be right back," said Gene, hurrying off through swinging double doors.

"So, is this Sir Kon famous or something?" asked Sara, her eyes back on the dwarves.

Calderon grinned and answered, "He is in his own way. As I said, he is the leader of the city guard. Also, he is one of the largest men I have ever met. Sir Kon seems to be friends with everyone, though. He acts very much like a big kid, very unlike his brother, Sir John." Calderon grinned at a memory of the two brothers arguing. Kon was always the jolly, carefree giant, while John was straight and strict.

He came out of his thoughts to see Kyle frowning and staring at the three deserter Kusarkus, who were still deep in conversation. They were at a table not far from them, so it wasn't too hard to hear their voices. The one who had waved at Calderon seemed to be in charge, but all three were in bad shape. Their clothes were travel-worn, and even their horns, which most Kusarkus took good care of, were gouged and chipped, as though they had been butting heads. The thought gave Calderon a cruel chuckle. Serves the dirty traitors right, he thought grimly.

Then some of the words the leader Kusarku was saying registered. "We keep doing what we're doing. I don't care what others say. I say we are better off on our own than under a pointed-eared thumb. Or worse, under the tottering of the half-breed Bard."

Calderon's temper was rising, and he tried to shut out the Kusarku's voice. Now, though, it seemed to buzz in his ear like a determined bee.

In a deep voice, the Kusarku continued, unaware and unconcerned, "If Bard had his way, he'd sell his own kin just to make ends meet. Hell, I'd rather be free and poor than the boot licker of elves." The other two laughed, throwing back their heads.

Calderon, now shaking with anger, made to get to his hooves and teach those traitors a lesson. However, as he started to rise, Kyle pulled him back into his seat and gave Calderon a meaningful look. Sara placed a comforting hand on Calderon's arm, and he swallowed hard and turned his face toward the hearth.

Looking into the fire, he was soon lost in thought. Bard had done his best with a bad situation. "Sometimes there is no right choice," he had told Calderon. There are times when any choice you make will have bad consequences somewhere down the line. What being a leader was about was making the tough choices and making the best you could out of your choice. I hope that one day I can be half the leader Bard is and that I can make the right choice for the right reason. Even if others don't understand my reasons, Calderon thought. He glanced back at the deserters, wishing he could give at least the one who was speaking a good, solid punch.

Calderon hated deserters because, to him, they had abandoned their own people. He didn't believe that disagreeing with the way things were being done was grounds to leave. If you disagreed with something, you didn't just run away. You stayed and did your best to make things better. To Calderon, the reason his people were so weak was because of disgruntled Kusarkus abandoning their people like the three at that table had done.

Taking a few deep breaths, Calderon forced himself to get control. Kyle and Sara were right: fighting those three idiots wouldn't solve anything. Looking back around at his friends, he forced a smile. He couldn't think of anything great to say to break the monotony, so he just said simply, "Thank you."

"Don't mention it. Not worth the effort, you know. Plus, I think our food is here," said Kyle.

It was indeed, for as Calderon looked up, Gene was walking towards their table. In his hands, he carried a tray with three steaming bowls and three mugs of some dark liquid. He put a bowl and spoon down in front of each of them, followed by the drinks.

"What is it?" asked Kyle, his eyebrows raised.

Gene crossed his arms and smiled. "It's bean soup, of course, with ham. Can't you see that?"

Kyle frowned a little while picking up his mug. "No, I meant the drink."

Gene's grin widened. "Well now, that's my specialty. It's made with sassafras root. Try it before you turn up your nose at it."

The three friends looked at each other. Then together, each took a small sip.

"This is great, and it even smells good," exclaimed Sara. The other two agreed happily.

"I'm glad you like it. Make sure you pass word along to others about our food and drink here. Now, dig into that soup before it gets cold. I'm sure you will find it to your liking as well. I'll check on you all in a bit." Then Gene turned and hurried back behind the bar.

Calderon blew gently on a spoonful of soup and took a bite. It was as delicious as the drink, maybe even more so.

The chunks of ham were soft and salty, and the soup broth itself was very savory. There were several types of beans along with chunks of tomatoes and carrots in it too.

"Remind me to thank Sir Kon," said Kyle between mouthfuls. "I'll make sure I do the same."

"I didn't know sassafras was used in drinks. I've only ever heard of it being used in medicine," said Sara while taking another drink.

Both Calderon and Kyle agreed. The drink was good, rich tasting, and smooth at the same time. Calderon exhaled with exultation. Kyle took another gulp and burped loudly.

Sara looked at Kyle, amused. Calderon, feeling his own belch coming on, inhaled deeply and burped louder. The three of them broke up, laughing.

Sara sighed, saying, "This is nice. Most bars and taverns in the Gold Dwarf cities get a bit crazy."

Calderon nodded. He had heard that when dwarves drank, they drank hard.

Gallagher's had a pleasant, relaxed feeling. To Calderon, it was hard to believe that a place like this could be in the same world as the unrest and nervousness happening in other places. It felt like this village was a safe haven where cares diminished and time slowed to a crawl.

They continued eating and drinking while Sara told them a story of one of her and her father's adventures. They had made their way to Stormbreaker Mountain and to the site of the great battle that had ended the Grey War. "There was this uneasy feeling there, as though you were being watched. If any place is haunted, it's that place. You could see where explosions had torn the ground. Even though many people have scavenged the battlefield for weapons and armor, my pa still said you could find things there. And he was right. We found swords, daggers, axes, and arrowheads."

She smiled to herself. Calderon and Kyle ate their soup and didn't interrupt her reminiscence of her father. Calderon thought of his own fond memories of Bard showing him trade manifests and supply orders. They had made such lessons into games. Bard would give Calderon a paper showing the breakdown of their current supplies. Then Calderon would circle the goods that were most needed in their kingdom. Though it may not sound like fun to others like Kyle or Sara, to Calderon, it had been enjoyable. It had felt good when he found something and even better when Bard rewarded Calderon with treats.

Kyle cleared his throat, breaking Calderon's reverie. "Something is going on," said Kyle, gesturing with his chin toward the bar. Gene, looking wild-eyed, was hurrying from behind the bar and in their direction. Calderon tensed and clenched his fist.

Gene hurried over and, to Calderon's surprise, bent to whisper into Calderon's ear. "I've got a room upstairs with two beds. It's the second door on the left. You three have got to get up there. I won't have friends of Sir Kon's injured or worse in my tavern."

Calderon gave the old man an alarmed look, and Gene nodded

gravely then rushed to add, "A Dwelling Elf just came and warned me. Three elves just entered town. They are going from person to person, asking after a group that fits your description. I don't know what they are about, but I'd wager it isn't to wish you well."

Calderon nodded and got up quickly. "Thank—" began Calderon, but Gene cut him off.

"Just get yourselves out of sight."

Calderon nodded and motioned for his friends to follow him. Although looking confused, they did so without question, hurrying up the old stairs that creaked mercilessly and through the door to the second room on the left.

Calderon quickly put down his pack and crossed to one of the two beds in the chamber. Sitting down on the straw-filled mattress, he looked up at his companions, who were giving him questioning looks from the doorway, where they still stood. Gesturing frantically for them to follow him into the room, he whispered as quietly as possible, "Sit down, quick, and don't make noise. Some elves are asking after us."

Kyle and Sara looked at each other and then did as Calderon said.

Kyle sat down on the edge of the bed next to Calderon while Sara sat on the other bed, facing them. The beds creaked loudly as they shifted their positions. Calderon winced at the sound.

Kyle leaned forward, asking in a whisper, "Who do you think it is?"

Calderon shrugged. "I have no idea, and honestly, does it matter? They were asking after us, and they're elves, so I doubt they mean to wish us well."

Sara nodded. "Maybe someone blabbed from your home, Calderon. Or maybe someone saw us on the road."

Calderon frowned at Sara and said, "I don't think anyone in Dreadston would be a traitor. Anyone who would go against Bard would already have deserted our people, like the ones down there in the tavern."

Kyle nodded, asking, "What do you think those three deserters will do when the elves come in?"

Calderon chuckled darkly. "Probably run away with their tails between their legs."

Sara frowned at him and asked, "Why do you hate them so much? They're Kusarkus too."

Kyle and Calderon both looked at her as though she had grown a second head. Her comment had taken Calderon aback. He didn't know how to put his feelings into words. Kyle seemed to be dealing with the same issue for he held a finger up as if to make a point but couldn't start.

Finally, Calderon said, "It's just personal. I wouldn't abandon our people just because I disagree with the way things are run. If you don't like something, you do your best to make things better. Does that make any sense?"

Sara nodded slowly. "I understand, I think. They say the dwarves split into two factions because they couldn't agree on how things were done."

There was a loud clatter on the stairs, and all three friends stiffened. Calderon hoped no one had told the elves they had been there. He thought about Gene; Gene wouldn't say anything. He thought he had read the man well enough to tell that Gene could be trusted. Plus, there was Kon. If Sir Kon trusted the place enough to send Calderon there for food and shelter, it must be okay.

Sara drew her feet up onto the bed. Then, trying to ignore the uneasiness about the elves finding them, she pulled her braid over her shoulder and began to mess with the golden knots. Kyle was staring at her. Noticing Calderon's gaze, Kyle blushed and looked away.

Calderon let out a sigh. "I guess we should try to relax. I'm sure we are safe here." He spoke with what he hoped was a confident tone.

Sara smiled at Calderon hopefully then gave him a questioning look. "Are you able to use your magic to see what's going on down there?"

Calderon nodded slowly and shrugged his shoulders slightly. "I can try. I might be able to use a mirror or something as a kind of window to the first floor."

Looking around the room, he saw that it was simple in its furnishings. However, there was a small dresser with a good-sized mirror hanging over it. Calderon concentrated hard on the mirror, putting a picture in his head of the room below. Nothing happened at first, so Calderon pushed his concentration harder. Then the reflection of the bedchamber began to swirl in the mirror like water running down a drain.

When the swirling ended, the mirror instead held a view of the room below as seen from the mirror that was behind the bar. That wasn't a true mirror, though—just a reflective surface of polished brass. Therefore, the picture came back to them tinted and a little distorted, but they could make out the scene well enough.

All three shifted on the beds, causing the rough wooden frames to squeak again. The room appeared the same as before, except for the three elves that now stood in front of the bar. Two of the elves, wearing bored expressions, were tall and straight. Their dark hair was short, showing off their large, pointed ears to full effect. The last elf was shorter, with light brown hair. His nose was hook-shaped, as though it had been broken and not reset properly.

All three wore tattered traveling cloaks of a faded olive-green color. The short elf appeared to be talking to Gene. However, Calderon couldn't hear anything being said. The mirror projected only the likeness of the room, not the sounds within it. The elf displayed a sardonic expression, as though he either didn't believe or didn't care what Gene was saying. Calderon glanced at his friends.

Kyle grinned at him and whispered, "Nice one, Cal."

Calderon gave Kyle a wink and focused again on the mirror. It was hard to maintain the focus to keep the spell going. A bead of sweat rolled down the back of Calderon's neck.

A flurry of movement drew their attention to the three Kusarkus, who were now standing. The Kusarku leader was saying something loudly. In fact, Calderon could actually hear the muffled voice through the floor. All three elves turned in the Kusarku's direction, and the small elf said something in return with a sneer. As the elves turned back to Gene, another of the Kusarkus rushed at the elves. The tall elf nearest to the Kusarku turned and, with the speed of a cobra, struck the Kusarku twice, once in the belly and once in the temple. The Kusarku crumpled out of sight.

Calderon and his friends heard the three elves laughing from downstairs. Calderon clenched his fist, and the glass's image began to swirl and distort as Calderon lost his concentration. Kyle put a hand on Calderon's back. Calderon again centered his mind on his task. Slowly, the image came back into focus to show the elves exiting the tavern through the main doors. As the doors closed behind the elves, the other two Kusarkus hurried forward to help their friend. The humans went back to their drinks while casting the door and Gene worried looks. The Red Dwarves hurried over to the Kusarkus and began gesticulating at the door.

Calderon couldn't see the expression on Gene's face or know what he said. However, the old man appeared calm as he filled tankards for the dwarves and Kusarkus. With many backward glances at Gene, everyone took their seats.

With a sigh, Calderon let go of the magic and laid back on the bed. His head hurt from concentrating on the magic so hard for so long. He felt like a smith was pounding on his head with a hammer. Opening his eyes, he saw his friends standing over him with worried expressions. He smiled at them despite his headache.

"I'm okay—just overdid the magic a bit," said Calderon.

His friends' expressions relaxed.

"At least, whoever they were, they didn't find us," said Sara.

Kyle nodded his agreement, saying, "That old man really came through for us."

At that, there was a soft knock at the door. Before they could do or say anything, Gene came in, closing the door behind him. At first, his face appeared grave, but when they met eyes with him, he smiled, the wrinkles around his eyes and mouth becoming more prominent.

"Well, you most certainly came to the right place. Them elves was lookin' for ya, but we sent them on their way," said Gene.

Calderon smiled, thinking better of saying he had seen it all. Instead, he asked, "What did they want?"

Gene shrugged. "They didn't say. Only asked if there was a group like yours here at the inn. They gave a description which matched yours well enough."

Calderon frowned, scratching his chin. Not for the first time, he wondered who was after them.

Gene shrugged his bony shoulders again. "Just know they are good and gone. You can stay the night, of course. And don't worry over anyone tonight. We here in Crescent like travelers, especially when they pay. But we won't have troublemakers in our town."

Kyle and Sara sighed audibly.

Calderon stood up and put out his hand. Gene shook it; Calderon could feel the strength in the old man's fingers. "We appreciate everything you are doing for us even though we ourselves are strangers." Calderon let go and reached for his money pouch.

Gene, however, shook his head. "You just tell Sir Kon to stop by sometime, and we are even. I owe that giant, anyway."

Calderon thanked him happily, and Sara and Kyle added their words of gratitude as well.

Gene laughed and made his way to the door. "Just let me know if you need anything else." They all thanked Gene again, and he left.

"This Sir Kon must be quite the human to get us free food, drink, and lodging," said Kyle.

Sara nodded, leaning back on the bed and stretching. She kicked off her boots and laid out on the bed fully, though she barely took up half the length of it.

Calderon smiled. "Sir Kon most certainly is something. But you can make your own opinions when we meet him tomorrow."

Calderon and Kyle began to undress to just their pants. On a table were a large blue bowl and pitcher. They had a few spare clothes they could change into, so they went about cleaning the dirt of the road off their arms, legs, and faces. The water was cool and refreshing.

Then Sara cleared her throat. "When you two are done, go over and look out the window." They did as she asked and kept their eyes on the scene outside. "And don't let me catch you two peaking at me, or I promise you will be sorry."

Calderon finished drying himself on a spare towel. He smiled as he thought, We aren't watching her, but she sure did watch us. Calderon felt a twinge of curiosity as he stood at the window. The thought of sneaking a peak made him blush and grin guiltily. As Kyle stood beside him, Calderon saw that Kyle was red faced too. Wondering if Kyle had the same thoughts as he did, he continued to direct his gaze outside.

There was no sign of the three elves that had been following them. Darkness was falling over the town of Crescent, and a few humans were moving on the street below, going about their last-minute chores. A rather plump woman walked into view and entered the inn. A moment later, she came out scolding her drunk husband, her shrill voice breaking into the night air.

"I sure hope that doesn't end up being us one day," said Kyle, and they both laughed.

"I'm all done," Sara announced. "Why don't we turn in early?"

As Calderon turned away from the window, a large bird flew by. Calderon didn't think anything about it—just an owl out for a nighttime hunt, he figured.

It wasn't an owl, but it was hunting in a way.

Sara lay in bed already, her knees drawn up so the bed looked like it had a small tent. "You boys did good this time, but don't let me catch ya tryin' something." Her tone sounded harsh, but she said it with a smile.

"Don't worry. I've been taught to be good," joked Kyle. The three laughed, and Kyle and Calderon crammed into the second bed. Kyle's long legs took up a lot of space, and Calderon kicked him. Kyle kicked him back, and the two smiled.

"No playing footsies, boys," joked Sara.

When their laughter trailed off, the three young travelers relaxed into the creaking beds. The mattresses were kind of lumpy, but the sheets were soft, albeit somewhat threadbare. Happy that nothing had gone wrong so far, the two Kusarkus and one dwarf drifted into a much-needed sleep.

Chapter 11

In the middle of the night, Calderon awoke suddenly. He lay still with eyes closed, listening. Kyle lay next to him, breathing the slow breaths of someone deeply asleep. One of Kyle's legs was spread out, pushing Calderon's legs to the edge of the bed.

Obviously, Kyle is a bed hog, and he must have kicked me, trying to get more room, Calderon surmised. Getting comfortable again, he relaxed.

Then, from the bed next to theirs, he heard Sara thrashing about. Without thinking, Calderon got up as quietly as he could and went over to her. Sara was rolling this way and that in a fitful sleep. In the bright moonlight streaming through the window, he could see her brow furrowed in apparent discomfort. Not knowing what else to do, Calderon placed a hand on her shoulder.

Sara jumped, and her eyes flew open to pierce Calderon. One of her hands was raised to strike. In a moment, she blinked, and her look changed from one of alarm to understanding and then to sadness. She sat up and turned her face away from Calderon.

"Are you okay? What's up?" asked Calderon gently.

Sara kept her face averted, now looking toward the window, looking anywhere, apparently, other than at him.

She was silent for a minute then answered softly, "I'm fine, Cal. Just a nightmare."

Calderon moved to comfort her—how he didn't know. Just his impulses seemed to direct him. Before he could hug her or something, anything, she shook her head.

"Please. I'm fine. Like I said, it was just a nightmare. Really. Go back to bed. We both need our sleep."

Calderon felt that she was right but also thought it wrong not to help. Feeling deflated and unneeded, he said simply, "You know I'm here if you need to talk."

Sara nodded, and as Calderon turned away, he saw her wipe her face. As she did so, he saw she held a piece of red woolen cloth.

Getting back into bed, Calderon made himself comfortable. He closed his eyes and tried to relax and find sleep again. As he did so, he heard Sara whisper, "Thank you, Cal." Calderon smiled to himself and pushed Kyle's leg back to his own side of the bed. Still grinning, Calderon relaxed completely and let sleep take its hold over him.

When Calderon next awoke, Kyle and Sara were shaking him.

"Time to get up, Cal. Come on, come on, come on!" said Sara, positively bouncing. She looked like a child excited to open her presents. Calderon couldn't see any remnants of last night's distress in her eyes. Kyle was dressed in a different traveling tunic, this one blue. His horns and hair shone in the predawn light coming through the small window.

Calderon rubbed his eyes and sat up. "Is it time, already? Are you two sure you're ready to hit the road?" Calderon asked the two of them and smirked, knowing the answer already.

In response, each grabbed one of Calderon's arms and pulled him from the bed. Calderon laughed, and the other two laughed too. Sara walked to the window and looked out so Calderon could change. He put on a tunic the color of mountain fir trees. Then he put his weapon's cuff on his wrist. The always-cold metal made him shiver. Grabbing up his pack, he announced, "All right, then. Let's go."

Kyle snatched up his own bag, quiver, and bow. Sara bounced over to her boots, pulled them on, and hurried to the door. Calderon and Kyle smiled at each other and hastened after her. Once out on the street, they looked around. It was mostly empty but for a few people just beginning their day. A woman was carrying a large bucket to the town well. The dog from yesterday was playing fetch with a stick. The brown hound's large ears flopped up and down so hard as it ran that Calderon thought the dog might take flight.

Feeling considerably better after a good night of rest, they left the small sleepy town. The woods were much the same as the day before. Squirrels ran all about their business, sometimes barking with irritation at people below. The cooing of mourning doves could be heard along with the twitterings of other birds beginning their day.

Sara stretched her hands to the overhanging branches with obvious delight. "It's going to be a great day," she said then looked over her shoulder at the two young Kusarkus, arching an eyebrow playfully. "Last one out of the forest is a troll booger." With that, she bounced forward, her blond braid flying back behind her.

"Well, I'm not gonna take that lying down," said Kyle, and he laughed, bolting after her. Calderon grinned and leapt into the race.

However, just as they set off, enemy eyes were already on them.

Kyle, with his long legs, easily outran both Sara and Calderon. Calderon came in second, but it was a near thing. Sara moved fast on her short legs, making Calderon go all out. The pack on Calderon's back didn't help, but that was just an excuse. All three were sweating from their exertion.

Taking a deep breath, Sara said, "Well, I guess I'm a troll booger. Oh well. Next time, I'll remember to trip Kyle when he's off balance."

Kyle flushed deeply, but Calderon chuckled. Kyle, in his attempt to win, had tripped over a loose stone at one point, nearly causing him to fall. Turning away to the path, Kyle clenched his fist, obviously frustrated. Calderon took a deep breath to stifle his mirth and gestured for Sara to follow him. She sobered, seeing that Kyle was upset. But Kyle turned to his friends, swallowing his vexation, and gave them a slight smile.

The road before them rose up a large green hill. They couldn't see the land around them well.

Calderon slapped a hand on Kyle's back and said, "Take the lead, Kyle, and get a good look around when you reach the top of the hill. We don't want any surprises, and you have the best eyes."

Kyle nodded to him, not smiling, but Calderon could tell he was pleased all the same. He hurried up the hill, obviously taking the job seriously. Calderon and Sara followed more slowly.

Calderon kept looking over his shoulder at the woods behind them. Whereas before the trees had felt protective, now they seemed menacing.

Seeing his nervousness, Sara nudged him. "Stop worrying. I've got your back, Cal."

Calderon gave her a grateful look. "I appreciate it. You can always count on a dwarf to have your back." That said, Calderon couldn't help taking another backward look. All he saw was a hawk fly out of the woods. It circled overhead and then flew off in the direction of Alezadria.

As they reached the top of the hill, Kyle turned and smiled at them. "It looks all clear, sir," said Kyle, striking a mock salute. Calderon gave him a salute in return, grinning.

"You both are dorks," said Sara. Both Calderon and Kyle broke out into laughter.

Stopping to look at their surroundings, Calderon saw a familiar sight. The hills rose and fell in green waves with the road running through them. A few fellow travelers could be seen here and there. In the distance, a larger hill than the others jutted up like a small mountain.

Calderon pointed to it and said happily, "We are almost there. That is the man-made hill before Alezadria."

Kyle blinked in surprise as they resumed walking. "How is that man-made, and why?"

Sara answered, "The idea is that the hill will slow an enemy. You can set up your forces either on top of the hill or on the other side of it so the other army won't be ready for you."

"More designs of Landon's?" asked Kyle.

Calderon shook his head. "No, it's far older. I was told it was designed by a human king long ago."

Kyle shook his head, also. "Humans really are amazing, aren't they?"

Calderon nodded and smiled to himself at a memory. Calderon thought, They have no idea. They haven't even met King Adam, yet.

King Adam had greatly impressed Calderon, and his magic power was tremendous. People were always impressed with Calderon's magic, too, but Calderon thought he only looked like a paltry magician next to King Adam.

Soon, they had reached the big hill. Calderon kept scanning the area, but he saw no threats. There were more people than ever about them. However, everyone seemed to mind their own business.

Sara pulled on Calderon's arm. Pitching in, Kyle did too.

"Let's go, Cal. Come on," Sara said anxiously.

Giving them a small smile, Calderon let go of some of his trepidation and ran up the hill. Sara hurried ahead while Kyle and Calderon followed.

The grass around them was a sea of green and yellow. As they reached the top of the hill, they were all out of breath from the exuberance of their reckless run up the steep slope. Breathing hard, the three looked out over the city of Alezadria below them.

Now that they had reached the top of the hill, they could easily see their destination. Only a half mile away stood the huge wall that encompassed the city. Calderon heard Sara say in awe, "It is fifty feet high by twenty feet thick, made of granite by our king and master stonemason, Landon."

Kyle looked in wonderment at something so big and with so many people going in and out of its massive double wooden doors.

Calderon smacked a hand on his friend's back and forced a nervous smile. "We didn't come all this way to just look at the wall," Calderon said happily. Then, more quietly he added, "Remember to blend in and stay calm." And with that, he turned and started down the hill.

As far as the eye could see, everywhere was green and blooming. Bard had said that the mountains to the east and west of the valley lands kept everything verdant and growing most of the year.

Sara spoke up again, offering information like an encyclopedia. "The granite was taken from the Grey Mountains and was placed so perfectly that no one can find any handholds to climb the wall."

Kyle spoke up as well. "The walls are so tall and the hill so steep that an enemy would be easy pickings for good archers."

Sara snorted. "Archers," she scoffed as she hurried up next to Calderon.

Calderon hoped his short horns didn't draw too much attention to him. Even the other races would stare at him because of them, sometimes. Also, Kyle's and Calderon's hooves were loud on the now well-paved road beneath them. As they walked, they passed three hooded people, apparently refugees, on the right side of the road, and a large, muscular man sat on the hill nearby, facing the city. The man looked very familiar to Calderon.

Suddenly, Calderon felt a firm hand placed on his shoulder and a stern voice said, "Whoa there, strangers. And where might you all be going?"

Calderon jumped and quickly turned. The three refugees stood before them. All three were travel-worn, and Calderon noticed with trepidation they all looked like elves. Without a doubt, Calderon suddenly knew it was the elves that had been looking for them in Crescent.

"We heard King Adam was offering support to refugees," said Calderon, half turning to move away.

Kyle was standing stiffly, though, looking like he was ready for a fight, and even Sara had moved forward toward the three strangers in a defensive stance.

"We heard the same," said the smallest figure, who lowered his hood. He was handsome, with brown hair and bright green eyes; his nose was bent slightly as though it had been broken before. Yes, it was definitely them. Then, with sudden earnestness, he leaned toward Calderon's trio and said in his high voice, "We have been waiting for people just like you. Come with us now!"

The two elves flanking them reached inside their robes, gripping something suggestively—probably swords or, more likely, daggers. Kyle raised his fists and lowered his head, ready to fight. Sara leaned into a fighting stance as well. Calderon raised his left hand, ready to cast magic, but he couldn't think what to cast. Should the spell draw attention? Should he not try to hurt these elves?

Then a gruff voice cleared his throat behind them. Calderon grinned to himself. He had been correct about who the large human was. The three elves released what they were holding and shuffled toward who was behind Calderon. Calderon turned and saw with relief that it was Sir Kon, Leader of the Guards of Alezadria.

Kon was a huge bear of a man with scars on his arms. His shoulder-length hair and beard were dark brown. He wore no armor but for a shirt of chainmail that covered only his shoulders and chest over a worn leather jerkin. His only identification was a necklace with the human kingdom's coat of arms, a gold dragon on a red and blue background on a small circular plate. He gave Calderon a half wink then turned gruffly to the three elves, who began to state their case.

The elf who had spoken to Calderon spoke to Kon in a high voice that sounded like he was trying to sweeten. "Please, sir, we are humble wanderers seeking shelter from your lord. To whom do we have the pleasure of speaking?"

Calderon's brain thought of a question: why did his voice seem unnaturally high and abrasive? Most elves had musical, pleasant voices that made Calderon want to sleep.

Sir Kon said nothing but turned to the city walls and held up his right hand. Something flashed in the sun's light. As if in answer, there was a great roar. From behind the wall rose a green dragon, which flew quickly in their direction. The use of dragons as mounts had become common since even before the Grey War. It was said that amiable dragons had been necessary to fight off wild dragons and monsters with no names that had once stalked the land. However, only green, blue, and gold dragons allied themselves with the two-legged races. The other dragons—the red, black, and copper—weren't so friendly.

Calderon wasn't surprised and gave a hint of a smile. Sir Kon had always liked making an impression on people. Kyle and Sara were moving nervously backwards and stopped when they were next to Calderon. However, their apparent uneasiness was nothing compared to the frightened reaction of the elves, who, Calderon could see even from behind, were shaking like saplings in a thunderstorm as the dragon with a rider on its back flew up and landed just behind Kon. The sunlight glittered off the dragon's scales in shots of green.

Kon now turned and leered at the elves. With one hand held out, palm up, he said, "I am Kon, Leader of the Guards of Alezadria. You will release all weapons to me now. Threatening refugees of any race is not permitted on our lands. Will you stay, or will you go?"

The three elves said nothing but hurriedly handed over three daggers and then all but ran past the dragon with not many backward glances as they went on their way.

"Getting up to trouble as usual, eh?" said Kon with a booming laugh as he walked up and pulled Calderon into a hug. Calderon felt like his ribs would crack and could feel himself blushing.

"And I see you still handle things by making your grand impressions," quipped Calderon, glancing at the dragon and rider.

The dragon, Calderon noticed with a little trepidation, had been staring at him with its yellow eye since it had landed. It seemed to be listening as it looked at him, as if expecting Calderon might bark an order at it.

Kon laughed again. "The dragon? Yeah, I thought she could use the experience of being on guard. She and her rider, Kara, are new to the ranks. But tell me, who are your friends?"

Still staring at the beautiful dragon and trying his best to meet those intimidating eyes, Calderon relaxed. He introduced Kyle and Sara. Sara was clearly excited again, but Kyle was still pale as he looked at the dragon and rider. Green dragons like this one came from the Dark Woods. And although riders did patrol the Grey Mountains, they had seldom come to Dreadnot. Now that Calderon thought about it, there had been a strange lack of dragons and riders on their journey.

At once, the dragon's head snapped around, and it blew a puff of smoke at a hawk circling overhead. The hawk screamed in fright and flew off. Then the dragon turned back to Calderon with what Calderon thought was a pleased expression. Calderon smiled at it but inwardly wondered what was up with this dragon.

"Off with you now, and do your perimeter check in two hours," said Kon to the dragon and Kara. Kara saluted, and the dragon took off, the wind from its wings buffeting the group. Again, Calderon couldn't help but notice the dragon's gaze upon him until it turned back toward Alezadria. He wondered if he looked like food to the dragon even though it wasn't yet fully grown.

As they began to walk towards the city, Sara began to heap questions on Kon, like, "How many people does it take to man the city wall and doors?"

Kon laughed, answering good-naturedly, "We have patrols spread out on top of the wall. Each patrol takes a guard tower and has to deal with their stretch of wall," he added, pointing to the nearest guard tower.

"What about the Archers' Guild? How many archers do they supply?" asked Kyle, getting over his fear.

Kon smacked Kyle on the back. "Ah, an archer, are ya? Yes, each patrol has at least four archers from the guild, though every guard can shoot a bow of some sort, whether it be a bow or a crossbow."

As his group reached the doors spread wide for them, Calderon was so relieved to be back in Alezadria. While the doors, a rich russet, looked huge from afar, up close they looked gigantic.

"They're made of oak that has been treated with a special oil made by us Gold Dwarves," said Sara proudly, seeing Calderon gazing at the doors.

"Those planks must have been from huge, old trees. Just imagine the stories they could tell," said Calderon as he continued to gawk at the structures. He thought for a moment how sad it was that something so big and old had died to give refuge to others. Then again, at least their death and use had come with purpose. The doors were each at least twenty feet tall and thicker than a man with his arms outstretched.

Sara didn't answer. She was staring up at the wall itself. Every stone fit together so precisely you couldn't even slide a piece of paper between two of them. Just as Sara had said, no one could scale the walls by hands alone.

Sir Kon turned to the six ground-level guards as one of them hurried up and saluted him, taking the daggers and hurrying away to the guardhouse.

"I still need to watch for a few more hours. We have to make sure we look our best with so many people coming here. Anna, here, will take you to the castle," said Kon, grinning at them all and smacking Calderon on his back, nearly knocking him off his hooves.

Calderon and his friends thanked him. "We will catch up at dinner," said Calderon as Kon hurried off, waving as he made his way inside the guardhouse.

The trio turned to Anna as she stood in front of them. Anna, a human with red hair, looked about their age. With countless freckles covering both cheeks and across the bridge of her nose, she was shorter than Calderon by about an inch. As with all the guards, she wore light armor with the human sigil on her breastplate. Unlike the other soldiers, though, she bore a small shield and a short spear.

Anna smiled, gave a quick nod of her head, and straightened her back. "I'm Anna, as Sir Kon said. I grew up here. I'll get ya to the castle real quick with no trouble," said Anna in a contralto voice, low for a girl, though it was still pleasant sounding. They each nodded in return and thanked her, and Calderon gestured for her to take the lead.

As they moved through the city, Calderon noticed townspeople as well as travelers wore swords and daggers with new familiarity. He asked Anna quietly about it as they walked around a large group of people at a street market.

She nodded with a grim expression. "There has been trouble here just like everywhere else. People aren't so trusting in days like these. You saw back there, though, if anyone draws a weapon on someone, we take it from them."

Kyle curled an eyebrow. "So, you can have a weapon but not draw it? What's the point?" Calderon and Sara nodded in agreement.

"I've heard it's an idea that if you have a weapon, people are less likely to draw theirs on you, but that doesn't always hold true. I have to say crime has gone down, though, so what do I know?" Anna said with a nervous laugh, as one does when they don't know if what they said was a joke or not. Catching herself, she straightened her shoulders again, looked forward, and said in a more formal tone, "Right, then. This way."

Anna turned onto a side street, seeming to be aware of the rest of the group's unease in the big crowds. She was right. Though Sara and Kyle were excited to see the city after their long journey, being surrounded by so many people all at once was a bit shocking. Now that they were on a quieter street with almost no other people, the four, including Anna, seemed more relaxed.

Anna had appeared tense at first but now began to talk to them in a more casual tone. "I don't see many Kusarkus 'round here. Where are you all from?"

Kyle piped up happily. "The Grey Mountains, near the Pyrite River and Stormbreaker Mountain. Do you know where that is?"

Anna shook her head sadly. "No. I've never been out of the valley lands and not too far from Alezadria, at that."

"Kyle and I have never been outside the Grey Mountains until now," said Sara helpfully.

Anna nodded at Calderon. "And what about you, Calderon?"

Calderon smiled nervously. "I actually lived in Alezadria for a time when I was training at the castle."

Anna whipped around with excitement. "What was it like? Who taught you? Why come to Alezadria?"

Calderon laughed and looked away, hoping he wasn't blushing. "I came and learned from Sir Kon, his brother Sir John, King Adam, and other members of the court the king deemed appropriate. It is what my adopted father, Bard, wanted." Calderon looked back at Anna. She looked at him with her mouth agape before hurriedly putting a more dignified look back on her face. Calderon hoped Sara wasn't making an "Oooh, you are soooo special!" face at him.

Kyle luckily caught that it was awkward for Calderon—who never liked to be seen as getting special treatment—and cleared his throat. "How much further is it to the castle, and which way do we go?"

Anna seemed to shake herself and pointed. "It's this way," she answered and turned to the right down another small side street.

To keep the conversation going as they went along, Calderon asked, "How long have you been in the military?"

Not looking back this time, she answered, "I've only been in my current spot for a few moons. I only just finished my training in the yard. It's a real honor to serve under Sir Kon." Then her face fell momentarily, and she muttered something under her breath Calderon didn't catch.

Calderon moved up so he was walking next to her, and he noticed she was grinning ear to ear, now. Calderon smiled too. It was nice to meet people like Anna, and it didn't hurt that she was pretty, either. Looking at her, Calderon thought back to Molly at home and felt himself go red. Soon, they took a left and entered an alley that was well lit by lanterns hanging at the back doors of many shops.

Suddenly, the group stopped and listened. From further down the alley, they heard sounds of a struggle followed by a loud crash and then silence. They looked at one another. Anna seemed to be about to head in the direction of the noise when one of the shop doors flew open, and two men appeared, carrying a large wooden trunk between them.

Anna nearly shoved her charges behind some large crates in front of a nearby shop. From their hiding place, Anna and the others cautiously peered down the alley at the two men.

The men laughed, and one said as he closed the door behind him, "Did you see how the old man went down when I hit 'im?"

The other one said, "Yeah! Went down like a tree," and they laughed again. Both looked down the alley in the direction away from Calderon's group. "Where's Jack? We gotta get the goods out of here before someone sees us."

"He said to wait for him, right?" the other man replied as they stood there, holding the trunk, continuing to peer down the alley.

"We can take them, right, Calderon?" asked Sara quietly.

Calderon nodded and gave Anna what he hoped was an easy smile, like he did this every day. "Listen, I have a little magic. If you want them to surrender easily, I'll blind them or something so you can get in close."

Anna nodded, but she still looked pale, and even Kyle looked a little unsure.

"I'll back you up. Don't worry—we girls gotta stick together," said Sara. Anna gave her a grateful smile and turned back to the thieves, who were still looking expectantly down the alley in the other direction.

Anna adjusted her shield and stepped forward. She stamped the butt of her spear on the cobblestone. "Halt there, you two, and surrender at once!" Anna commanded. For all of her trepidation, she sounded completely sure of herself.

The two men jumped and dropped the trunk with a loud thump and turned to face her. Their faces, which at first had been nervous, now split into confident grins as they laughed to each other.

"I said surrender and drop any weapons," ordered Anna, raising her shield to a ready position.

The two men only pulled out two wicked-looking daggers and made their way toward her. Anna seemed worried, now, so Calderon motioned, catching her attention, and then gave a quick nod and smiled. She nodded back then ran forward, shield extended and spear at the ready. Calderon pulled on his magic and focused the light around the two thieves so it shone straight into their eyes.

"Ahhhhh! What the—" yelled one of the men as they both stopped dead in their tracks and covered their eyes.

Anna, in six quick strides, crossed the distance between herself and the enemy. She slammed her shield into the face of the first man. He went down hard on his butt. Anna pivoted, swinging the butt of her spear around to knock the knees from under the second man. Flipping the spear in the air, she pressed the point to the man's chest.

"Surrender! You two are beaten," asserted Anna, breathing hard.

The first man gave a wild cry and lunged towards Anna's legs, but Sara ran up and punched him hard in the temple. The man went down again as his eyes rolled up in his head.

Kyle laughed from beside Calderon and hurried forward to join the girls. Calderon followed suit.

"See? You had that. You barely needed us," said Kyle happily.

Anna nodded. "I appreciate it. We can turn these two over to the other guards at the castle."

Calderon looked over at the chest the men had been stealing. He couldn't help but think it looked familiar. It was made of mahogany and displayed the symbol of a morning glory on its lid. He inwardly shrugged to himself.

Then there was a bang, and they all jumped as a small man with sandy hair and beady brown eyes flung open the back door of the shop and nearly fell into the alley. Calderon thought he resembled a mole.

"Ah, you caught them! Thank you!"

Anna recognized the man. He was the shop owner, and his name was Clyde. "Have you been harmed?" asked Anna.

"No, no. Just a bit roughed up. I don't know what I would have done if they had gotten away with that trunk. You there," he said, directing his gaze to Kyle. "Help me carry it back in."

Kyle looked around as if the man was talking to someone else. Then, he stepped forward and helped the man pick up the box.

The man grumbled a word of thanks and then nodded again to Anna. "Thank you kindly, guard. I'll let your superiors know what you did here. For shame if those two had gotten away with that chest. And in the middle of the day, no less."

"We are here to serve, as ever, sir," answered Anna automatically. Then the man hurried off with Kyle, the box between them.

Sara looked perplexed. "So, the castle guards also keep order in the town?"

"Yes," Anna answered with a shrug. "It is important to King Adam that his people are safe, so we don't just protect those who live in the castle."

Sara looked impressed at that, and Calderon agreed. That was part of the reason Calderon respected King Adam so much.

Soon, Kyle returned, a puzzled expression on his face. But Sara and Anna didn't notice as they were busy binding the men's hands behind their backs. Anna had put the men's knives into a rucksack she carried on her own back. The thieves said nothing to them, still looking around as though they expected someone else.

"What's wrong, Kyle?" asked Calderon.

Kyle shook his head. "He's just a shopkeeper selling a bunch of old stuff. What could be special about anything in there, I don't know. He acted like that trunk was some kind of treasure chest."

Calderon frowned in thought, but by now, everyone was on their feet.

"Off we go, then. What were you two saying?" asked Anna as she took the lead, the thieves walking before her with their heads down.

"Nothing. You did really well back there. Are you sure you're new?" asked Calderon.

"Thanks! I guess growing up with three older brothers prepared me well. Makes you tough," Anna replied.

Sara let out a laugh. "Brothers? Try growing up with sisters. Girls play dirty."

They all laughed at that, and soon, they walked into the broad daylight of the town square. The bustling square held many stalls where people sold their wares. Towering over them were several churches festooned with gargoyles looking down, ever watchful upon the scene below. At one end of the square was a huge gate and beyond it, the castle. Many races inhabited the square, but the majority of people were human, of course. Calderon fondly remembered going to this market and others on days when he could sneak away from his training for a bit.

Anna led them expertly through the crowds to the main gates. The Castle beyond seemed to shine in the sun like a jewel.

"Must be made of marble or something, and it's well polished," said Sara softly.

Calderon had not been there for two years, but at the sight of the castle, tension in him seemed to loosen. The castle of Alezadria, though large, wasn't a thing of beauty like some of the other castles he had seen depicted in paintings and illustrations. With the wall as the primary defense, the castle was built to be a last stronghold, fortified through years of labor. It had only two large towers, with the rest of the castle consisting of a large complex of rooms and halls.

At the gate stood at least twenty guards, their plate armor glinting in the sun. All bore spears and wore longswords belted at their waists.

Anna pushed the prisoners towards the guards saying, "Caught these two trying to steal from old Clyde." She pulled the daggers from the bag and showed them to the other guards. "They pulled these on me when I asked for their surrender."

One of the guards stepped forward while the others remained at attention, sweat beading on their faces. He was tall and straight, clean shaven, with a longsword on his hip. Unlike Kon, he wore a white tunic. His brown hair was pulled back into a ponytail that hung to his shoulders.

It was Sir John, Kon's brother, who had helped to train Calderon. Now, however, as he was in front of his troops, he made no acknowledgement of Calderon's grin in greeting.

"Guard," he said, speaking to Anna, "you will return to your post. Mason, take these two away."

Anna saluted, turned away, and smiled knowingly at Calderon and his friends. Then she whispered, "I'll meet ya later. I owe you guys big. Sir John is a bigger softy than Sir Kon—trust me," she said to Kyle, who looked nervous, then hurried off.

Sir John grumbled then, "It's about time you got here, Calderon. Come on. Don't just stand here with your mouth open like a gasping fish."

As the gate was opened, John led them inside and up to the large wooden doors. You could have walked a dragon through them.

"We are glad you made it through without trouble," murmured Sir John quietly. That was John's way: berate you in front of people and hide everything else behind a facade. Sara and Kyle were talking together as they followed, walking through the doors and into Alezadria's Castle.

Chapter 12

As THEY ENTERED the great hall, Sir John turned on Calderon abruptly and said harshly, "Where in the Seven Kingdoms is your weapon? Haven't I told you time and time again to always carry protection?"

Calderon stepped back hastily into Kyle, who cursed and fell over.

"I have a weapon, but it's . . . complicated," said Calderon, producing his sword from under his shirt. "I kept it concealed because I thought it might draw too much attention," he continued quietly.

John's eyebrows rose at the sight of the weapon as he bent slightly to take in its unique form. "Ahh. Bard finally gave it to you. Well, it's about time. And how's it working?" asked John, straightening up again.

"Yeah . . . wait—what do you mean 'how is it working?'" asked Calderon.

John, though, was now looking at Kyle and Sara. "And who are you two? Calderon's bodyguards or what?"

Kyle spoke up. "Well, uh, sir, I'm Kyle. I came along to help Cal travel, sir, and we met Sara on the road, and, uh . . ."

At that, Sara interrupted: "They met me outside Eldall. A troll had grabbed me. Calderon and Kyle saved me, and I owe them."

John hissed, "Not so loud. Keep your information about trolls and such for King Adam's ears alone." He took a breath and added, "But I'm glad you all made it here unharmed."

He gave Calderon and his sword another curious look. "You must get cleaned up, first. We can't have you getting road dust all over the castle." With that, he called over one of the pages and instructed, "See to their rooms and have them taken to King Adam as soon as possible."

The page nodded and answered softly, "It shall be done, sir," to John and then turned to the travelers and added, "Please follow me."

Soon, Calderon was enjoying a very welcome hot bath. A few cuts on his arms, which he had gotten while running through the trees from the troll, stung as he scrubbed himself. He washed his hair then sat back and relaxed, his thoughts turning to the events of the past few days and John's comments about his sword. What could be so special about this weapon?

Calderon hadn't thought about it at the time, but now he wondered: how had the small blade so easily cut off the troll's fingers? There had been little to no resistance, like a hot knife going through butter. Wait, he thought. Hot—hadn't the blade been hot? How had that happened? He shook his head and said aloud, "I'm sure King Adam will know something. Maybe I'm just tired." He splashed some water on his face, stood up, and stepped out of the tub. He began drying himself and combing out his hair before pulling it into a ponytail, imitating Sir John's style.

Looking through his bag, he came across some nicer clothes he couldn't remember packing. Probably Bard had been looking out for him. He shook his head and murmured, "Old habits die hard, Bard. I have to grow up someday. Well, at least they will do." He donned the soft linen tunic, dark blue with the Kusarku sigil, and tan breeches that fit well. He looked at himself in a mirror; yes, they would do. He put the weapon's scabbard on his belt and wound the chain around a belt loop so the length of it hung down his leg. He fastened the wrist cuff on and headed out into the hallway.

Sara and Kyle were waiting for him with the valet, who stood waiting attentively with his hands joined behind his back. The man was short and stocky with close-cropped blond hair and bored brown eyes.

Sara had changed out of her traveling clothes and now wore a fawn-colored dress with a simple forest-green surcoat. Her golden hair hung in loose waves with only the top pulled back into two small, interwoven braids. Calderon wondered where she had gotten the clothing. Then again, Alezadria was a big city. It was easy to find clothes here of all sizes.

Kyle wore a nice tunic and breeches similar to Calderon's, but he looked uncomfortable. He kept pulling at the tunic's lacings and glancing at Sara, who was looking out a window at a courtyard below.

"If you all will follow me," the valet stated, "King Adam is expecting you for dinner."

The valet then turned and began walking quickly down the hallway. Sara and Kyle gave Calderon a look. He nodded, and the three hurried after the older man, trying not to run to keep up. It was difficult. Though the valet didn't look like he should be, he was very quick-paced, and soon, the three were gasping with all the stairs they were climbing.

"Where are we going?" piped up Sara.

The valet slowed and turned to say, "We are going to the king's private dining hall. I've heard you are his honored guests tonight." He gave a small bow, turned on his heels, and continued climbing, albeit at a slightly slower pace.

Finally, the valet stopped outside a single door in a well-lit hallway. He gave a deep bow this time, opened the door, and ushered Calderon, Kyle, and Sara inside.

King Adam sat at the head of a small rectangular table. To his right and left sat Kon and John, and behind the king, standing straight in military precision, stood Anna. King Adam wore a white robe with purple accents. As ever, he held his gnarled staff. When Calderon and his friends bowed, King Adam stood up, his hands wide and welcoming.

"Calderon, Kyle, and Sara, I'm pleased you all have arrived safely. I welcome you to my table. Please join us for our repast, and then you may tell us of your journey here and of what happened near Eldall."

Calderon stepped forward and sat at the end of the table opposite King Adam. His friends sat near him. "It's so good to be back, your highness. It's a relief to be able to help in any way I can," said Calderon.

Sir Kon stirred. "So, little Cal, how are you liking Torin's weapon? Is it working well? It looks good on you."

King Adam frowned. "We will talk about that later. What's important now is dinner." He smiled then and raised his right hand. White light lit the table. When the light disappeared, food of all kinds now covered the table's surface. Kon and Kyle leaned forward and began to eat with gusto. Sara followed suit. King Adam and Calderon met eyes. King Adam gave him a fatherly smile, and Calderon smiled in return before digging into a roast chicken. It tasted so good, and soon, grease was running down his cheeks. He wiped his face, hoping no one noticed.

In between generous bites of baked potato, Sara asked, "So, this food is magic? But it tastes so good; how can that be?"

"It had better taste good—it came from our kitchens. But a magician never reveals all his secrets," said King Adam before adding confidentially to Sara, "It's how I stay one step ahead."

Sara laughed and speared a porkchop onto her plate.

Kyle was talking animatedly to Sir Kon of his dreams of joining the Archers' Guild. "I know the guildmaster, Jiren. I'm sure I can set up a meeting," said Kon, happy as a fox.

Kyle grinned from ear to ear. "Really? I am humbly grateful, Sir Kon."

Calderon then cleared his throat and asked, "Will Lady Julia be joining us?" He tried not to appear hurt. Julia was King Adam's adopted daughter. She also happened to be Calderon's friend.

The King raised one heavy white eyebrow and answered, "As I understood it, she said she didn't want to be stuck in a room with boring old men." He laughed, allowing his head to roll back.

The rest of them laughed as well, except Kon, who muttered, "I'm not that old."

"You are too that old, Sir Kon. If you looked any older, I'd say you needed to retire," came a giggling voice from the doorway. It was Julia. She skipped irreverently into the room, wearing a simple outfit of brown breeches and a purple tunic.

Rising hurriedly to his hooves, Calderon started to bow to her, but she broke into a quick run and hugged him tight, making him blush.

When she let him go, he laughed nervously, looking at her as she introduced herself to Kyle and Sara. Julia was just as Calderon remembered her—a petite elf with dark brown hair styled in a loose braid. She had very white skin and eyes the color of the deep ocean. Julia was as carefree as ever. Skipping over to King Adam, she hugged him and took a seat beside him that appeared out of nowhere as she sat down. King Adam's eyes were full of amusement.

"Now, I believe you were all in conversation before I decided to make my grand entrance," said Julia. "What did I interrupt?"

John answered her, "We were just about to discuss Calderon's journey here, and you were already listening at the door, I'm sure."

Julia smiled at Sir John, her father's trusted Lord Marshall, commander of his troops, without a trace of embarrassment.

"Your highness, will King Landon be here as well?" asked Sara hopefully.

"Of course. We would not hold this council without the king of the Gold Dwarves. He sent word that he was looking forward to attending," answered King Adam.

Sara, acting younger than her years, positively beamed and almost wiggled with excitement.

Suddenly, John caught Calderon's eye. "Tomorrow, before the council convenes, you're going to show me what you've learned with Torin's weapon. You okay with that, little Cal?"

Calderon bit back his nervous desire to say no and answered, "Of course. I've been practicing a lot."

"Speaking of which, why don't you tell me the whole story from the night you came across the strange dwarves until now," said King Adam, leaning back in his chair.

"Yes, Calderon. Do tell," said Julia with anticipation.

Calderon let out a nervous breath and began. He told everything he remembered and did his best to not omit any details. For the most part, they all listened without comment.

Kyle was pleased when Kon raised his eyebrows in surprise when he heard of Kyle's skill in shooting both the dwarf and the troll. However, the men's reaction to Calderon's mention of his weapon's mysterious sharpness and its feeling of heat perplexed him. King Adam, John, and Kon looked at each other, at that point, with grim faces. Even Julia had a crease in her brow.

King Adam nodded when Calderon finished his tale. By now, the food was gone, and servants had brought in goblets of fine elven wine for each of them.

"You've done well thus far, but don't set your sights low. All of us have the ability to reach for the stars and do things we imagine are impossible. Remember your training, and when in doubt, always go back to the basics to support you."

Calderon nodded although he was troubled by King Adam's words.

"He's right, you know," Sara said quietly aside to Calderon. "Even with all your training, did you ever imagine you'd fight a troll? Yet you and Kyle did—and saved me," Sara added, touching his arm gently.

Calderon flushed and took a sip of his drink to cover his embarrassment.

"That's enough for tonight, though, everyone," said the king. "We should all get some sleep. You three have had a long journey and have a challenging day tomorrow."

The three friends stood up and bowed, saying their thanks and good nights. Julia gave Calderon a mock bow; she always made fun of such proper decorum.

Sir John and King Adam both stood up, smiling, but Sir Kon walked with the others toward the door.

"Don't let my brother beat you black and blue tomorrow, Cal," Kon said. Calderon tried to smile but felt like his jaw was tight. "Speaking of training, you two should train too. We have all types of weapons for dwarves, and, Kyle, I'll see if I can have ol' Jiren stop by to observe you."

He winked, and Kyle stammered, "Th-thank you, Sir Kon."

Kon only chuckled and raised a hand as if to say, "It was nothing."

As they turned to leave the room, Calderon caught Anna's eye, and they both smiled. Calderon heard King Adam saying, "So, young lady, I hear you did well today. Tell me, do you want to serve your king in—"

but the king's words broke off as the door was closed.

Outside, the same valet was waiting to lead them back to their bedchambers. The trio of friends didn't talk much on their way back. Calderon was thinking over what had been said during dinner and trying to figure out what had been implied. What was so special about his weapon? What was it? He needed answers; maybe he could get Sir John to open up tomorrow during their sparring match.

Just then, Kyle broke in on his thoughts. "Can you imagine it? Me, actually in the Archers' Guild? I mean, I always wanted this chance, but I never thought it would really happen."

Calderon nodded and smiled at his friend's exuberance. "It is fantastic, but I always knew you were good enough. Are you excited too, Sara? I mean, it's not every day you get to meet the leader of your people." She nodded, smiling widely and yet nervously. "What's wrong?" asked Calderon, lowering his voice.

Sara looked at him sideways. "It's just . . . I never thought I could be telling other races a secret of my own race. Does that make me a traitor? We weren't telling other races about our troll problems, so am I jumping ahead of my fellow dwarves?"

Calderon shook his head, and Kyle put an arm around her. "Listen, tomorrow we will request an audience for you with King Landon before the council convenes. That way he will know and won't be taken aback when he hears our account of what happened during our travels."

"Right," said Kyle supportively.

Calderon gave Sara a comforting smile and explained without concern, "Of course, I met King Landon when I trained in Alezadria, and he and my foster father are old friends. It'll be just fine."

Sara looked somewhat relieved and nodded thankfully. "I'm glad I came with you both."

Kyle and Calderon laughed amiably. The wine at dinner had put them in a good mood, and after a moment, Sara joined in. Looking up, Calderon noticed they had arrived at their bedchambers, and the valet was bowing to them.

"I will, of course, sirs and madam, have someone awaken you in the morning," said the valet stiffly but not unkindly.

Calderon thanked him and turned to his friends. "Well, let's all get some rest in real beds and be ready for tomorrow. What do you two say?"

His friends enthusiastically agreed, and they all wished each other a good night and went into their rooms. Calderon stripped out of his tunic and sat on the edge of his bed, holding his father's blade before him. Tomorrow would be a big day. He would finally learn how to use the weapon. "I hope Sir John knows about this weapon and knows what he's doing. I'd hate to end up hurting him because I don't really know how to control it yet."

Putting the sword and chain on his bedside table, he lay down and pulled the soft blanket over him. He saw how the moonlight from his open window shades played across the sword's wave patterns. In that silvery light, it almost looked alive. Calderon sank deeper into the soft, luxurious mattress—filled with down, he suspected. After days of being on the road, it felt wonderful. Soon, he was fast asleep.

In the morning, he was awakened rudely by something poking him in the face. At first, he thought nothing of it and tried to go back to sleep. He was so warm and comfy. Then he was poked again, and he remembered where he was. As he realized someone must be in his room, he rolled hurriedly out of bed.

However, as he turned, his hooves caught in the blankets, and he landed flat on his face. Calderon heard someone laughing hard from above him, and he forced his eyes open. In front of him were two very small feet in sandals. Calderon raised his eyes upward and groaned; it was none other than Neb, a Dwelling Elf.

Dwelling Elves were the smallest race in the Seven Kingdoms. They were largely seen as a nuisance by many of the other races, for they often liked to cause trouble and mischief. Neb was no exception to the rule, even though he was said to be a leader of sorts of the Dwelling Elves. That was according to Neb, at least.

"Well, little goat, did you find something you dropped?" joked Neb, laughing again. Calderon struggled to get his hooves untangled from his bed sheets as Neb continued to guffaw. "Always sleep with one eye open, lil' goat, or always be surprised. Do you ever learn?"

Finally getting his hooves free, Calderon stood up and got a prompt elbow to the gut that sent him back to his knees. "See? The same tricks always work. Lord, if I were ever so blind, I'd be dead," said Neb as he vaulted over Calderon and landed lightly on the bed.

Grumbling, Calderon got up again and stared hard at Neb. "What have I done to deserve the pleasure of your visit so early?" asked Calderon, rubbing his stomach.

"You should get much worse for not coming to see me when you arrived," answered Neb, relaxing on Calderon's pillow.

Calderon began to dress and answered honestly, "I didn't know you were here, and I had to report to King Adam."

"I'm always around and watching," said Neb darkly. Calderon shot him another piercing glance.

Neb was wearing pastel colors in a green shirt and blue breeches. Around his left shoulder was slung a belt of pockets that hung to his right hip. Neb had mahogany hair, a chubby, good-natured face, and bright hazel eyes. Calderon knew from experience his pockets were full of trinkets, small instruments, and sharp, deadly knives.

"Anyway, what are you doing here, Neb?" asked Calderon.

Neb blew out a long breath. "Watching over you, of course," he said evasively.

Calderon shook his head, unbelieving.

"Do you know why we Dwelling Elves are known as one of the Seven Kingdoms?" asked Neb seriously.

Calderon again shook his head. He didn't know. He'd often thought of it as a sort of charity.

"It's because we keep the other races honest," Neb explained. "Trust me, there will come a day when a Dwelling Elf will have your back while you never even knew they were there."

Calderon looked away, hoping Neb didn't see his disbelief. How could anyone so small, and so . . . well, silly . . . do anything meaningful? pondered Calderon to himself as he laced up his boots.

Neb vaulted off the bed, landed cat-like next to Calderon, and ruffled the Kusarku's hair. "I'll see you at the council. Don't let Sir John beat you too badly in the meantime," said Neb, skipping to the door.

Looking up with a smile, Calderon answered, "Good day, Neb."

Neb stuck his tongue out and said, "I'll just be sliding down the railing." Then Neb smiled, opened the door, and went out.

When Calderon finally got out into the hallway, he found Sara waiting for him. She wore a simple brown tunic and leggings, but they fit her well. Calderon smiled warmly, saying, "Good morning. Sleep okay? Is Kyle up yet?"

She snorted and smiled as well. "Morning, Cal. Yeah, he's up. I've knocked three times, but he keeps saying, 'Just a minute.' Seems to take as long as my mother to get ready."

Calderon rolled his eyes and knocked on Kyle's door, which was suddenly flung open mid-knock, and a disheveled Kyle almost fell out through the doorway. Stifling a laugh successfully, though Sara had been less successful, Calderon slapped Kyle on the back and asked, "I was starting to wonder if you were okay in there."

"I'm fine, I'm fine. It's just the bed was so soft I didn't want to wake up. Then I couldn't get my hair right or my clothes on properly."

Sara nodded and said with a shrug, "The beds are softer than I'm used to, so I just slept on the floor."

Kyle had on a green tunic that clashed with his brown breeches. His bow and quiver of arrows were strung over his back, and he touched the top of the bow self-consciously. Calderon, reminded of his own training ahead, felt a hint of butterflies in his stomach.

Sara, though, skipped in front of them and said, "This is going to be a big day, so put a move on it, you two." Following her lead, the other two hurried after her down the stone staircases to the main floor.

Sirs John and Kon were there waiting for them. Kon held a mug of something steaming in his left hand. John was grim and nodded at their approach.

"Good timing, you three. We are just about ready for the day's training. It's this way," said John, waving an impatient hand over his shoulder as he walked to the east hallway and training yard. Around the yard were warriors of all shapes, sizes, and races.

On the yard's left side, archers fired steadily at straw dummies while a wiry man in well-used leather watched on.

"Come with me, you two. I'll get you all set," said Kon, putting a heavy arm around Kyle and nodding to Sara.

Calderon wanted to watch his friends go, but his eyes were transfixed on John, in front of him, who had drawn his longsword. John then tossed two small boxes to Calderon. Inside one was a sticky lacquer, and in the other, thick pieces of cotton.

"Put that on the edges of your blade. I don't need you taking anyone's body parts off with wild swings. But remember to keep control—cotton will only do so much, so you still need to be careful," said Sir John as Calderon guarded the edges of his sword.

When Calderon was prepared, he got into a ready stance and nodded. John jumped in, stabbing forward with the speed of a diving falcon. Calderon barely dodged out of the way then cut at John's leg, trying to get him off balance. However, John had already backed up, using his longer blade as an advantage. He began to rain down blows on Calderon, always staying out of range of Calderon's blade.

Calderon backed and parried as quickly as he could, attempting to send John's blade out wide so Calderon could rush past John's guard. Frustrated and trying to throw John off his footing, Calderon stabbed forward with his sword but let go of the handle so that it shot forward, point first, at John's hip.

John knocked the sword easily away and then leapt in, kneeing Calderon in the stomach. The young Kusarku fell to his knees, gasping, all the wind having been knocked out of him.

"Don't get impatient. Keep your cool," John instructed, his stance at the ready again.

Letting out a slow breath, Calderon rose to his hooves and pulled the chain of his sword back in, winding it around his left arm. He had an idea. What if he used the chain as a shield? John grimaced and jumped back, swinging at Calderon's right shoulder. Calderon parried and stabbed forward, keeping John away. John stabbed three times. Calderon, barely repelling John's attacks, was quickly getting out of breath. If he was going to try a new tactic, then now was a good time.

As John swung at his left shoulder, Calderon blocked the blow with his chain-guarded arm and then jumped forward, stabbing at John's exposed left hip. John leapt back.

"Better, better. But can you keep that up?" said John with a slight grin on his lips.

John swung hard, and Calderon blocked again with his chain-covered arm. This time, though, it hurt Calderon himself as the chain dug into his own arm. Calderon winced, opening and closing his hand, trying to get feeling back into it.

"Remember, strike with full force. Don't just hit something with a glancing blow. That would be less of an impact," said John, almost sounding like he was goading Calderon. "Come on, kid. Torin could do better in his sleep."

Calderon was fuming as he recklessly jumped in, slashing at John. In his frustration, he willed his blade to cut through John's stupid sword. John went to block the blow, and their blades met. Calderon next willed his sword to win the contest. Suddenly, with a shower of sparks, Calderon's sword cut straight through John's as though it were a piece of straw. Calderon rolled to the ground with an abrupt and unexpected cessation of resistance. Looking around, he noticed his sword was on fire and the chain wrapped around his arm was red hot. He hurriedly dropped both, looking down at his arm, expecting burns. However, there wasn't a mark on him, and as he thought about it, he realized hadn't felt any heat.

He looked up at John for an explanation, but John, for the first time Calderon had ever seen, was grinning ear to ear. He held the rest of his sword, but where Calderon's sword had cut through, it looked as though it had been melted.

"I'll need a new sword, but you're ready for me to show you some moves your father used," said Sir John as he offered Calderon a hand.

"What was that? What the—" began Calderon, but John cut him off.

"Not here. People are looking. And others will explain."

John quickly disposed of his sword's remains, complaining loudly about shoddy smith work. Calderon, still numb, rose to his feet and retrieved his weapon, which appeared just like it always had. Calderon ran his hands over the chain, still expecting it to be hot, but he still didn't detect any heat. Even the grass the chain and sword had landed on was burnt.

So why didn't it burn me? And how had it burned at all? But John doesn't seem surprised. Does that mean he and others knew about this? What does it all mean? thought Calderon. He couldn't get answers to these questions now, however, for just as John had said, a lot of people were about and curious. It wouldn't do to draw attention to himself for something that was obviously a secret.

Throughout the rest of the session, John showed him in slow motion how Torin had used the sword's chain to wrap around swords as they came at him. He could then use the opening to his advantage.

"Torin did use the chain around his arm as a shield as well, but always as a deflection, never a straight blow," said Sir John.

They kept on for another hour before John finally said, "All right. Take a rest and wash up. Can't have you showing up to the council later today smelling like skunk."

Calderon went to find his friends over by the archers, where Kyle was firing at a dummy and Sara, using a shortsword, was sparring with another dummy.

From above the training yard, on an overhanging terrace, stood Prince Elian. He watched the proceedings below with a slight curl to his lips. He could think of at least one or two people who would be interested in this news. From beside the prince came a loud clearing of a throat, and he turned to see Eryn, his father's lackey.

The elven prince sneered and hissed, "I enjoy watching these children play at being warriors. Please help yourself. I'm sure even you can find something of interest that doesn't involve walking in my shadow." With that, the prince gave a short laugh and brushed past Eryn, even giving him a wink. He hoped Eryn would finally lose his damned self-restraint and take a swing at him. However, Eryn did nothing but stare down at the courtyard with a frown on his face.

After a few minutes, John looked up, met Eryn's cold blue eyes, and nodded imperceptibly. John then continued teaching the young Kusarku, who was their great hope for the future. Eryn frowned to himself; he wondered if the boy yet knew what he carried and how important it was. Well, he and the others would have to tell him everything they knew . . . and soon.

As Calderon and his friends made their way out of the training yard, he noticed Anna and waved. She waved in response then turned back to the other young woman knight she was talking to. It was the dragonrider from the gate. Beside her, the green dragon stood, along with a blue dragon of comparable size. Calderon wondered how he hadn't noticed the dragons earlier. As before, the green dragon's penetrating eyes seemed to bore into Calderon like a carpenter bee into wood. The new dragon stared at Calderon with the same intensity. As he gazed into the blue dragon's eyes, he thought there was a question behind the creature's stare. Turning hurriedly away, Calderon listened as his friends chewed over their own training sessions.

Apparently, Kyle had made a good impression on Jiren. He kept saying how Jiren had been impressed by his arrow groupings. Sara had met with King Landon, who she said was "even more impressive than the marvels he made." Apparently, King Landon had given her the shortsword she now carried as though it were her newborn child.

Calderon grinned. He guessed his own story could wait. It wasn't like he understood what had happened, anyway. He didn't really know where to start, so it was probably best to nail down King Adam after the council and get his answers once and for all.

Chapter 13

CALDERON PUT ON his best clothes, hoping they were good enough, and combed his long hair. When he looked at himself in a mirror, he saw a kid that wasn't fully grown staring back at him. Maybe that was because everyone had horns bigger than his, he thought. Moving to his sword, he clasped the cuff, strapped the sword onto his belt, and attached the chain to his belt as well. Taking a deep breath, Calderon turned and pulled his door open.

His friends were waiting for him, both looking nervous. "Well, we came all this way; we might as well see it through," said Calderon, hoping his voice was bright.

"I've got your back, of course," said Kyle, unable to completely hide a tinge of apprehension in his voice.

"That goes for me too. And remember, Cal, the Gold Dwarves stand with you, so just say what you've come to say, okay?" said Sara.

Calderon nodded, wondering if King Landon had told her that in their meeting. Calderon rubbed his hands together and led the way down the now-familiar hallway to the grand ballroom, where John had told him the council would convene.

Outside the large double doors, the three stood and paused for a moment. Four guards in gold-plated armor stood, two on either side of the doors. Calderon looked to his friends, and they gave him encouraging nods. As they approached, one of the guards pushed open the doors for them.

A loud voice announced, "Presenting Calderon, acting ambassador of the Kusarkus and son of Bard, Regent of the Kusarku Kingdom. He is accompanied by Kyle of the Kusarkus and Sara of the Gold Dwarves."

Calderon's gaze flew around the room, quickly taking in everything he could as though he would have only one chance to do so. The room was enormous, at least eighty feet long and thirty feet wide. In the middle of it stood a long rectangular table made of rosewood. On the walls, banners hung alongside the human coat of arms, under which resided King Adam's personal sigil, that of a phoenix.

Calderon saw nine seats at the table filled, so far, with representatives of the various races. Behind some stood personal guards at attention. These, Calderon knew, were for a show of strength as well as protection. Calderon and Kyle walked forward, their hoofbeats echoing loudly on the highly polished marble floor.

Upon hearing Calderon's name, those at the table turned to look at his little group. King Adam sat straight and strong in a large ornately carved wingback chair at the head of the table at the far end.

Calderon, Kyle, and Sara walked a few steps further into the room. Each said, "Your Majesty," while the two Kusarkus bowed and the young dwarf curtsied.

King Adam smiled, his eyes flashing with amusement, and said, "I am pleased to have you attend. Please join us at the table."

As a servant led the trio to their seats, he whispered to Calderon the identity of each person at the table. Calderon saw that on King Adam's right and left sat Sir John and Sir Kon, respectively. Both were silent but nodded to Calderon in greeting.

Next to Sir John sat two High Elves. One was Prince Elian, who was there in the king's stead. Elegantly handsome, with long blond hair and piercing blue eyes, he sat tall and straight in costly-looking white robes trimmed in blue. Looking coldly at Calderon, who bowed deeply, he nodded dismissively in response. The other elf was Grand Chancellor

Eryn, according to the servant, acting as the prince's assistant while also representing the king. Eryn looked long at Calderon before looking down at some papers he had before him.

As Calderon and his companions walked on, two dwarves met Calderon's eyes. One, seated to Calderon's left, was King Landon. When Calderon began to bow to him in deference, Landon smacked him hard on the back and said, "Aw, come on, lad. We don't need that ceremony between us."

He, of course, had a wealth of blond curly hair that hung to his strong shoulders. Unlike the beards of most dwarves, however, his was short and well cared for. Landon's eyes were chips of flint, but they were friendly and surrounded by lines of laughter. He indicated the dwarf seated next to him and said, "And may I present his majesty, Dragol, King of the Red Dwarves."

Calderon instinctively bowed to Dragol, and both dwarves laughed. "Doesn't listen very well, does he?" said Dragol with a hearty laugh. Dragol looked to be quite a few years younger than Landon as no lines of age marred his weathered face. He had long, braided red hair and a beard that hung down his chest and across his shoulders. He was very muscular but covered in small burns. Both dwarves wore no crown and, indeed, were dressed only in simple, short-sleeved tunics.

Dragol laughed again. "Well met, lad. We've heard good things of you even in the Red Mountains."

Calderon smiled warmly. "I hope I get the chance to live up to those expectations." The man ushering Calderon cleared his throat, and Kyle quickly moved to their seats. Sara followed after her king and stood quietly behind him, but she smiled at Calderon when their eyes met.

Across from Calderon sat Duncan, wearing similar clothes to how he had dressed in the woods. He said, "Ah, finally, my friends have arrived. I got that package here days ago, and if I stay much longer, I might have to roll myself home," laughed Duncan. "I'm glad you made it safely."

"What is this about a package? There should be no secrets here," said Prince Elian grimly.

"It is no secret, and I promise all questions will be answered in their proper time," said King Adam pleasantly.

The elven prince harrumphed and looked away, speaking in a quiet voice to one of the three elven guards who stood behind him.

Calderon looked around the table again and noticed there were two empty chairs. He surmised that one was probably for Neb and the other for the leader of the Wood Elves, who rarely left their forest. Only one other person sat next to Duncan. It was Geshile. Calderon was told she was Queen of the Sobek; she nodded to Calderon when he looked at her. She had beautiful blue-green scales and bright orange eyes. A few of her pearl-white teeth showed from beneath her lips in a predator's smile. However, all of this was at odds with the sizeable spectacles perched on her overly large snout. She, unlike the other leaders, had no guards in attendance. The Sobek believed, Calderon remembered, that if a ruler needed protection, they were seen as lacking the strength to lead.

Calderon returned her nod and then he felt a hand on his shoulder. He looked around to find Anna standing behind him, grinning in her armor. She bent down beside him and said with a smile, "Don't worry. I'm right behind you guys—literally. King Adam asked that I act as your attending guard during the council." Calderon and Kyle grinned as well and thanked her before turning back to the table.

"Are we to wait here all day for the others?" asked Elian, stifling a yawn.

"Oh, were you waiting for me?" said a voice from behind the prince. It was Neb. He literally skipped to his chair. In mock sorrow, he said, "If I had known I was keeping your lordship, I would have run."

Calderon and many of the other guests had to fight to restrain their laughter. A dwarven guard behind Dragol was less successful and received a stony glare from the prince.

"Yes, yes, we are all here now. I've heard from the Wood Elves, who say they stand with the other races. However, they couldn't make it here due to their own situation," said King Adam.

Calderon and Kyle leaned toward Landon with questioning looks, for he had nodded, seeming unsurprised by the Wood Elves' absence.

Landon leaned close, whispering low through his beard, "I've heard that the Dark Woods itself has risen up against them, whatever that means. Keep me in a cave or tunnel rather than some spooky woods, I always say."

King Adam cleared his throat and nodded. "As to the attacks on each of our races, we are gathered here to share the information we have. We must dispel the rumors and stop pointing fingers. We must determine who is truly behind these attacks and why."

"Of course—once the rest of you admit that the Kusarkus are the ones doing this, that is. Their General Krasp was seen during some of these attacks. I've also heard the Kusarkus are siding with goblins," said Elian, his voice rising accusingly.

Kyle tried to jump to his feet in outrage, but Calderon pushed him back onto his chair. Calderon met Elian's eyes and said with forced calm, "General Krasp was exiled ten years ago. His actions have nothing to do with us."

"A Kusarku is a Kusarku, and I notice that there have been no reports of attacks on your race," argued Elian.

"Recent events may contradict that," said King Adam, drawing everyone's attention. "As I said, we should all come together here in the spirit of cooperation. It very well may be that an unknown enemy just wants us at each other's throats."

Geshile nodded her large head and said in her hushed, hissing dialect, drawing out each s, "There have been attacks on our rivers by monsters like hydras and even frog folk, with whom we thought we had an understanding. There was even an attack on our trade route at Snake River."

Dragol nodded, booming out in his baritone voice, "Our trade routes have been attacked, as well, over the valley lands and up the slopes. Trolls are becoming more common, and even the dragons seem to be stirring from their roosts." He and Landon both shivered at the mention of dragons, and even Calderon felt a spasm of fear run down his spine. The idea of large black and red dragons flying over the Seven Kingdoms was truly something to be frightened of.

"Anyway, what got your ear points in a knot, your highness?" Neb asked Elian.

Calderon thought he could hear Elian's teeth grinding together. Next to him, Eryn was staring between Calderon and King Adam, just as he had throughout the conversation so far. Calderon looked away hurriedly.

In a calm, controlled voice, Eryn said, "In a recent attack on the Wizard Headquarters, the High Wizard Stephon was taken along with, we think, Princess Elaine." At this, he looked down sadly. "We know from witnesses outside that goblins were seen attacking the guards. How they got all the way through the city undetected, we don't know."

"My sister is gone, and my father is ill, near death. I must act and lead my race into the future," said Prince Elian with a touch of his old arrogance.

Calderon himself felt sorry for both elves at the mention of the lost princess. It seemed to Calderon that each was simply dealing with loss in his own way.

Then Kyle burst out in sudden anger, "But it wasn't us. You can't just pick a race and point the finger and say we are to blame."

Prince Elian leapt to his feet in turn. "How dare you, dog! How dare you even have the nerve to speak to me!" The musical quality that usually pervaded the elves' voice was gone with his fury.

Kyle leapt to his feet as well, but Calderon put a hand on his shoulder, drawing him back into his chair as King Adam raised a hand.

Calderon felt his own frustration with and fury at Prince Elian. However, he figured the prince was just looking for an excuse to attack them. Maybe that was ever the prince's aim.

"I believe, before we accuse each other of anything, we must hear all the points," said King Adam firmly to Prince Elian and Kyle, giving both a penetrating gaze, which made Kyle shuffle uncomfortably but did not seem to have much effect on Prince Elian. Then, addressing Calderon, the king said, "I believe you have your own tales to tell us. Please proceed so we all may move forward together."

Calderon inhaled a deep breath and took a drink from the cup handed to him by a servant. Cool wine tasting of blackberries ran down his dry throat. Then, he began telling how he had planned his deer hunt and had gone to a clearing near Eldall. As Calderon spoke, his honest gaze scanning the group, King Landon met his eyes and gave him a nod. Calderon told everyone how, during his hunt, Duncan had entered the clearing where Calderon had set a snare and the two had met.

Duncan raised his own glass, amber liquid spilling over the sides in his exuberance. "I was there, sure as certain. I was working for . . . ," said Duncan before breaking off with a look at Landon.

Landon cleared his throat. "It is my understanding that, though it may be hard to believe, our people from Eldall and several other cities have suffered troll attacks."

Duncan nodded in agreement. "I found signs that trolls were indeed about, but I never found one of the monsters."

Calderon cleared his throat and continued, "While Duncan and I talked, we found we weren't alone." He then told how the strange dwarves had attacked. At the mention of the dwarves, both Landon's and Dragol's faces grew hard, their eyes flinty. "The one remaining," Calderon went on, "tried to throw a magical weapon, possibly a bomb. Lucky for me and Duncan, Kyle was watching from nearby and shot the enemy twice, once to kill and once to pin his throwing arm."

"And where is this weapon?" asked Prince Elian, unbelieving.

"More importantly, where is the dwarf that lived?" asked Dragol, looking between Calderon, Kyle, and Duncan.

King Adam said loudly, "Honored guests, the answer to your questions is that Duncan brought both here to Alezadria. I can have them summoned here at once for everyone's inspection, if you all wish it."

All heads had turned to King Adam, and Landon said tersely, "I think I speak for both our kingdoms when I say the dwarves would like to see this supposed dwarf; it is a grave matter that must be dealt with at once."

Dragol nodded his agreement, and Geshile hissed curiously, "I agree with the dwarves. I would love to see evidence of creatures that are working against us." Her great, long fingers thumped on the table, not in an anxious way, but as though she were playing a song on a piano.

Calderon looked across the table to the elves. Eryn was whispering to Geshile something about the movement of supplies on the great lake of Elizdiath. Elian's eyes were on the ceiling as he sat swirling his glass of wine.

For the first time, Calderon took closer notice of the elven guards. Unlike other guards, they wore full armor with helmets on their heads, complete with faceplates hiding their identities. They barely moved, so you could almost believe they were only empty suits of armor. Then a movement from King Adam brought Calderon's attention back to the room at large.

"My Leader of the Guards, Sir Kon, will bring us the dwarf immediately," said King Adam.

Kon bowed and hurried from the room. Once the door had closed, Duncan said, "Everything my young friend here has said is true, of course. Strangest dwarf I've ever seen, and I've been about."

"Be that as it may, how do we know this wasn't a plot to deceive the gullible?" said Elian.

"I don't agree. Such a thing, even if it were true, is not the Kusarku way," said Eryn, surprising Calderon—and Kyle too, from the look on his face. "I would hear the rest of your tale, Calderon, as we wait," continued Eryn.

Everyone else nodded their assent, and King Adam winked at Calderon.

So, Calderon told of them taking the "dwarf" to Bard and how Duncan had then taken him to Alezadria, to which Duncan nodded his agreement. Calderon didn't tell about his sword, however. He felt strangely protective of the information that it had been his father's and about the weird things it seemed to be able to do. Next, he told how he and Kyle had journeyed to Alezadria at King Adam's invitation.

"On our way, near Eldall, we ran into a troll that had captured Sara here," added Kyle. Everyone looked at Kyle, who tried to sink into his chair.

Then, as all eyes turned to Sara, she stepped forward boldly, tossing her blond hair. "That's right. They saved my life. I'd not be standing here if it wasn't for them. The blasted monster chased us all night till Cal, here, nearly cut the thing's hand off and Kyle shot an arrow in its eye."

King Adam grinned wide, and both dwarf kings laughed.

"That was well done, lads," said Dragol.

Landon added, "I owe you my thanks, also, because the attacks plaguing Eldall have lessened."

Calderon and Kyle grinned at the praise, and Anna whispered admiringly, "You didn't tell me you two fought monsters."

Calderon and Kyle both blushed, and Calderon changed the subject, saying loudly, "When we escaped the troll, Sara agreed to travel with us to bring evidence that weird things are happening all at once. Nothing else happened until we were waylaid by three elves in Crescent and then again outside of Alezadria."

At this, Eryn raised his eyebrows and shrugged. However, Elian threw his hands in the air and said, "We are managing the entire nation of High Elves. We can't control every elf throughout the Seven Kingdoms. I'm sure the rest of the leaders can complain of the same problems with people that take their frustrations out on others."

Indeed, several of the others nodded, including King Adam. However, for the first time, Sir John spoke up with sudden vehemence. "This wasn't an isolated incident of elves praying upon Kusarkus, and not just in the area of Alezadria. If this gathering does anything, I think it should encourage us to each inform our own people that these actions will not be accepted."

Raising his eyebrows at his Lord Marshall with an amused glint in his eyes, King Adam said, "I agree and will at least be following these measures. What say the rest of you?"

Looking around the room, Calderon smiled as each person nodded in turn—even Eryn, who gave Calderon a nod and small smile. Only Elian looked around the room before gritting his teeth and nodding as well.

In the quiet after the agreement, Kyle nodded vigorously, and Calderon kicked his leg. Sara and Anna laughed quietly, and even Landon and Dragol smiled. Then there was a loud knock on the doors, and they were pushed silently open. Sir Kon walked in, leading two guards who held the chained arms of the "dwarf."

Chapter 14

FOR THE FIRST time in days, Calderon felt himself relax completely, at least for a moment. They had successfully carried out their mission and delivered living proof of the strange dwarf who had attacked them. Any question that Calderon's story was a work of fiction was now in the past. The prisoner looked overall much better now than he had all those nights ago when Calderon had last seen him, although his nose was clearly broken and healing badly as the bruising on his white face stood out strongly.

His translucent white hair and beard were clean but seemed even more strange now in the presence of other dwarves who looked so vibrant and alive.

Duncan stood up, pointing at the "dwarf." "This is the dwarf, all right. I brought him all the way here, and an awful lot of trouble he was too," said Duncan bitterly.

Both dwarf kings stood as well, and for the first time, there was not a hint of a smile on either one's face. They hurried over to the prisoner, talking together angrily in Dwarvish, like two badgers arguing over a single hole.

Calderon only caught a few words of what they said but got enough to know that something wasn't right. Glancing at King Adam, Calderon saw he, too, was frowning but sadly rather than in anger, as though this were preordained to go badly, or as though he knew this council would cause this reaction but knew it was still necessary.

Suddenly, both Landon and Dragol broke into a run at the prisoner, and the guards closed the space in front of him. Landon and Dragol shook with fury, shouting at the guards in an unfamiliar Dwarvish language. The prisoner, like the other two dwarves, answered back angrily in the same language.

Kyle looked at Calderon, who shrugged in return, as bewildered as his friend.

It was Eryn, standing straight and tall, who asked the question in everyone's minds: "What is going on, you two? Get ahold of yourselves."

The two dwarf kings turned red in the face. Calderon thought he saw tears in Landon's eyes.

Dragol answered, voice shaking, "He's a dvergr, our sworn enemy. If there is one of them alive, then it is one too many."

"It's just like we suspected, Cal—a Dark Dwarf," whispered Kyle.

Calderon nodded. "At least we know what he is now and that there could be more of them."

Landon seemed to hear Calderon's whispered response, for he glanced at him and said, "You're right there, lad. We are even more in your debt now that we know the dvergar have returned before they could cause more mischief. And you there, Duncan. Take this for your trouble and for giving this bastard a few good wallops."

With that, Landon tossed Duncan a sack of coins, which Duncan caught. Grinning like a schoolboy, the troll hunter bowed low.

"But what mischief are they part of? We couldn't get anything out of this one," said Sir John, eyeing the dvergr with disgust as though he would like nothing better than to let the two kings at him.

"Well, let's ask him, shall we?" said Dragol, cracking his knuckles dangerously while glaring back at the dvergr.

At John's nod of approval, the guards moved aside, and Landon stepped forward again, talking in the strange Dwarvish tongue. The dvergr turned away, eyes and mouth closed tight.

Dragol leapt forward as well, and soon all three dwarves were shouting at each other, their faces scarlet. Calderon looked around the room. Most of the attendees were transfixed on the dwarves, and Sara looked nervous. Looking then at the elves, Calderon saw one of the three elven guards make a weird movement. The guard turned to the one next to him, who nodded in return. In an instant, the first guard drew a dagger.

Calderon shouted a warning as the guard threw the blade at the three dwarves, who quickly jumped out of the weapon's path. However, the dagger had still managed to slash Dragol's side as it flew by. At the same time, the other elven guard threw a glass sphere of swirling purple. It flew through the air and hit the main doors. A purple gas flowed outward, forming a large portal through which goblins poured.

There were at least a dozen of them wielding wicked swords and wearing patched armor. They were short with long arms that hung to their knees and putrid green skin. Their yellow eyes leered as they ran forward, attacking anyone in their way. Two ran towards the dwarves, who were now rising to their feet. Landon raised his fists in defiance.

Calderon heard fighting and struggles from the other side of the table. However, he had problems of his own as three goblins bore down on him and his friends. Calderon drew his sword and, drawing on his training, tried to make his sword heat up as it had when fighting John. But nothing happened, and he had to duck and parry as the first goblin swung at him wildly. Knowing he needed to attack, he blocked a thrust at his ribs with the chain and then cut at the goblin's exposed neck, but the goblin was out of his sword's reach.

Thinking back again to his fights before, he put all his will into drawing the sword's heat. Is this going to work? he wondered as the goblin swung at him again. Calderon's sword met the goblin's, putting a deep gouge in it. After a moment of resistance, Calderon's blade continued through, cutting the sword in two and then slicing the goblin across the chest. The goblin gave a gurgle and fell at Calderon's feet.

Looking up from the creature he had cut down, Calderon saw the other two goblins charging at his unprotected right side. He tried to turn in time to meet his foes but knew it was hopeless. Suddenly, a spear thrown from behind him caught the goblin on the right in the chest. Sara and Kyle then leapt forward, tackling the second creature and wrestling to disarm him. Calderon stabbed downward, ending the goblin's struggles. As the blood sprayed, Calderon winced and felt his gorge rise.

Swallowing hard, Calderon looked at his friends and nodded his thanks. "Let's split up and help the others," he said. Kyle and Sara nodded and ran forward.

Calderon hurried to Neb, who, with nothing but two daggers flashing in his little hands, was lazily sparring with a pair of goblins. Calderon, rather than going around the banquet table, leapt on top of it. Sending a drinking cup flying, he grasped the end of his sword's chain and threw his weapon to loop around the leg of one of the goblins. The blade barely missed the second of Neb's attackers. The goblin to Ned's right jumped at the sound of his fellow's shrieks of surprise as Calderon pulled his feet from under him. The goblin's legs blistered from the chain's heat. Neb took the chance and jumped forward quickly, thrusting his daggers into the other goblin's neck. Then Neb permanently silenced the second goblin's shrieks of terror and pain.

Calderon looked around the room and found Geshile had a goblin grasped in her jaws. With a violent shake of her head, she ended the goblin's struggles. Eryn was fighting the two elven guards who had started the whole mess. Elian stood behind them, taking in the room. Suddenly, he jumped forward, grabbed one of the guards, and threw him face first into the table. Just then, Kyle ran up and together with Eryn restrained the other traitor elf.

At the yawning purple gateway, King Adam stood, his arms spread wide. A bright green light seemed to emanate from him, and the purple mist vanished as though it had never been there.

Finally, all was calm. Calderon took a deep breath, willing his racing pulse to slow. Then, he realized for the first time that he was spattered with the blood of the two goblins he had killed. He had killed them. He felt sick to his stomach again and tried to wipe his arms clean on a linen napkin.

The doors of the hall banged open as human guards rushed into the room, swords and spears in hand.

Everyone was talking at once about the two traitor elves, who were now being restrained. Calderon paused, looking at the elf being held down by Kyle and Eryn, who had a black bruise blooming around his right eye. The traitor elf's face shield had slipped off, revealing a familiar countenance.

"Hey! Isn't that one of the elves that tried to attack us outside the city?" asked Calderon in surprise.

Kyle nodded, and Sir Kon walked over to them. He looked at the elf closely then nodded to King Adam and Sir John. When the elf began to struggle harder, John motioned to the guards and ordered, "Take them and secure them for questioning."

"They were your guards. Do have anything to say to that?" said Landon angrily to Elian.

"I don't like your tone, dwarf. Unlike others, I don't spend my days getting to know my underlings. That's why all my guards are masked. To me, they are only one thing—a guard sworn to protect me. That is normally all I need to know," said Elian haughtily.

King Adam cleared his throat. "Everyone, be calm. This could be a good thing."

"How could this be a good thing?" asked Geshile in a low hiss.

Calderon wondered that too.

"You see, we now know how enemies have been able to infiltrate our cities in such large numbers. Also, now that I've seen the spells they are using, I am sure I can find a counter spell that can dispel these gateways and prevent them from re-emerging, at least in the castle," said King Adam, the hint of a knowing smile appearing on his lips.

Calderon let out a sigh of relief and glanced around the room. The rest of the people looked relieved as well—all except for Elian, who for only a moment frowned and held clenched fists tightly at his sides. Then Calderon blinked, and Elian was smiling and thanking both Kyle and Eryn for helping to capture the traitors.

"As we have seen here firsthand, we have a common enemy, so I beg no military action be taken on our own allies. Now, we can form a joint plan of action. Please feel free to make use of my home as long as you like," offered King Adam.

Many began to move out of the room, some sore and wounded.

Dragol was holding his side with a cloth to reduce the flow of blood where the dagger had grazed him. However, he seemed to be all right. Everyone was talking about what had just happened and what they would do next. Indeed, the two dwarf leaders were deep in discussion with Geshile over a new trade route even with Dragol still bleeding.

Sara and Anna then hurried up to Calderon and Kyle. None of them had been hurt, and in seeing this, Anna sighed with relief. "I was right. If I stick around you guys, I will see a lot of action."

Kyle gave a wan grin along with Calderon. Making their way through the castle, they talked about the council and the fight.

"Did you see how well Landon fought with just his bare hands against those two large goblins while Dragol kept that Dark Dwarf prisoner? It was amazing. They didn't even seem to need our help when Anna and I got to them," said Sara with admiration.

"You should never underestimate a dwarf—that's always what Bard says," said Calderon.

"Yes, but did you also notice how Elian didn't do anything until the fight was decided?" whispered Kyle.

Calderon and the others frowned.

"I was hoping I was imagining it or something," he said.

"He is a flinty character. I've always been told, 'Don't trust an elf at your back,'" said Sara.

"Be careful, you three," Anna admonished in a hushed voice. "You never know who is listening."

As Calderon glanced around, he saw Eryn a short distance away talking to Neb of all people. "What could they be talking about?" wondered Calderon out loud.

Without pause, Anna answered, "Chancellor Eryn probably wants information from Neb, or else he wants Neb to tail someone discreetly."

Kyle and Sara looked at her, shocked.

Anna blushed. "I mean, it makes sense in either case. If you want something done quietly, you go to a Dwelling Elf, and Neb is the best around. It's not for nothing that he is known as the Speaker of the Quiet Folk," said Sara.

Calderon nodded. He had heard Neb called that before but didn't know what it meant.

Seeing the quizzical look on the others' faces, Anna sighed and explained, "Dwelling Elves, gnomes, and other such people do not have kings or queens. However, Neb was chosen by those races to speak and act for them."

As they moved off, Calderon wondered, not for the first time, how someone like Neb, so relaxed and full of pranks, could be such a trusted leader.

Kyle, however, asked, "Where do the Quiet Folk live?"

Calderon knew, but it was Anna who answered, "I've never been outside the valley lands, but Lake Elizdiath separates those and the dwelling lands, as they're called. They are supposed to be an area of grasslands that run right up to the Dark Woods where the Wood Elves live."

She all but whispered the mention of the Dark Woods and the Wood Elves as though they scared her. Calderon couldn't blame her for that; any place where something could be watching you just out of sight gave him the creeps.

As they left the great hall, Calderon still tried to look at anything but his hands or his weapon. The day was warm, but there was a strong breeze coming in from the east. Calderon noticed the gathering clouds as they passed a large window. They forebode a storm.

He heard the others talking of their future plans and wondered what would come next. Anna was saying something about coming by their rooms later.

Calderon tried to force a smile and keep his voice from shaking as he said, "Thank you all for everything. I'll discuss what is next with King Adam. I need to clean up first."

Turning, he hurried into his room and promptly threw up in a bucket.

Chapter 15

Stripping out of his clothes, Calderon flung them into a corner and began to wash himself vigorously from a wash bucket someone had brought while he was out. The chill of the water made him sputter and gasp, but it felt good, and he needed to get clean. He dried himself with a warm, soft towel and put on clean breeches. Suddenly, the gorge rose again in his stomach, and he hurried back to the waste bucket. He threw up hard, and when he was done, he felt himself covered in sweat.

He had killed something! Ended their lives. Calderon was living while they were not. Was it fair or just? He sat down on the edge of his bed and, staring out the window at the stormy sky, stayed like that for a long time—how long, he didn't know.

His eye caught a glint of something, and he looked in its direction; it was his sword, lying on the floor where he had dropped it. Calderon walked over and picked it up gingerly. He sat back down on the bed and looked at the weapon. It really was different from any weapon he had seen, and it was doing things he couldn't explain.

Where did the heat come from? Sure, he knew how it worked . . . kind of. Concentrating on willing the blade to heat, he watched as it and the chain steadily began to glow red in his hands. As usual, he didn't feel any heat from the weapon. Indeed, it felt cool to his touch.

Suddenly, there was a knock at the door, making Calderon start. Putting the cooling blade down, he adjusted his ponytail and said, "Come in."

Kyle and Sara came in grinning. Sara was carrying a bottle with some amber liquid in it, and on a tray, Kyle carried three plates of roast chicken.

"You've been in here for hours. You need something to eat," said Kyle.

"And we need to drink. We are alive, and we succeeded in our goal," added Sara, uncorking the bottle and pouring some of the strong drink into three mugs.

Calderon frowned. "Hours? Has it really been that long?"

Kyle nodded. "Only a couple, but you shouldn't sit in here all alone with just your thoughts."

"I'm with him. I don't like silence," agreed Sara loudly, as though trying to drown out a noisy crowd.

Calderon sat down on the one chair the room had and motioned for Sara and Kyle to sit on the bed. Taking a plate of chicken from Kyle and a mug from Sara, Calderon sat back in the small wooden chair, which creaked ominously, and took a bite of chicken. It was succulent, and grease ran down his chin with the first bite. He smiled at his friends and wiped his face. They smiled back and began to eat too.

Kyle said through a mouthful of chicken, "What do you think Bard would say of your table manners?"

Calderon gave a chuckle and said, "I'd argue that we don't have a table, anyways, so the manners are out the door with it."

They all laughed at that, and Calderon took a swig of his drink. It blazed down his throat, making him gasp. The drink tasted like strong dwarven ale mixed with whisky.

"What is that?" asked Calderon hoarsely.

Sara laughed, answering, "It's spiced rum from King Landon. He seemed to think we should celebrate."

Calderon let out a "Whew!" and took a second careful sip. "Well then, let's all drink up," he said, lifting his mug in salute to the others.

They did the same and both took drinks of the spiced liquor. Kyle's eyes were watering from the drink, but he cleared his throat, trying to appear as though nothing was wrong.

"I'm just happy it's all over. I mean, even though there was a surprise attack, it all seemed to work out," said Calderon, taking another bite of chicken.

His friends agreed exuberantly. "Honestly, I almost think the attack pushed everyone closer together," said Sara.

"I agree, but again, I don't trust that elf," said Kyle.

Sara raised an eyebrow at him. "You mean Prince Elian?"

Kyle leaned forward with a frown forming on his face. "Yeah. The guy seems to hate other people who aren't elves. During the fight, he didn't do anything until he saw which way the tide was turning. And I don't like how he always seems to be watching you, Cal," said Kyle.

Calderon smirked and said, "I'm glad I've got such an observant protector."

Sara snickered but Kyle continued to frown. "I'm serious, Cal. I've got good eyes. I've been watching him since we got here. Whenever we are around him, he's watching you."

Calderon understood Kyle's worry, but he didn't want to admit that he was worried about Elian as well.

Sara laughed harder as though unconcerned. "Next time I see him, I'll make sure to ask him out for you, Kyle," she said teasingly.

Kyle took a piece of chicken and bit into it as if it had done him a disservice.

"Anyway, as for what happens next, what do you two think?" asked Calderon, hoping to change the subject.

Sara looked at Kyle, and something passed between them in silent communication.

Kyle looked back at Calderon and said, "We've actually been talking about that with other people—asking what we should do now. Between myself and Sara, we agree that we should travel and do things around the kingdoms. You yourself, Cal, told me you hated being cooped up in the old castle."

Calderon nodded, smiling as the drink was starting to make his head buzz pleasantly. "What would Bard say, though? Don't they need us back home?" he asked.

"Honestly, what would we do there? They don't need us. We can do so much more out in the world," said Kyle. He put down his plate, leaned back on his forearms, then leaned his head back, stretching his neck as though it hurt.

Calderon found himself nodding. Kyle was right about that. What was he going to do at home that Bard couldn't handle? He nodded, throwing back his drink to finish it. "I guess you guys are right. I'll talk to King Adam and King Landon about where we could help best. I'm sure they have ideas. King Landon mentioned the dwarves housing the Kusarkus who are left at Dreadnot," said Calderon.

Both Kyle and Sara seemed to relax. Sara raised her glass, tossing her drink back as well. Her cheeks were red when she looked at Calderon as she rose to her feet.

"I'll go talk to King Landon for you to tell him what we've decided, give him some time to think, you know. Plus, I need to clear my head from this drink," said Sara, giggling as she made her way to the door.

Calderon nodded. "Thank you. I really appreciate you guys. But are you sure you're okay to go walking around in our state?" asked Calderon.

"Oh please. I'm just fine. I could drink you both under the table, no problem," Sara said with a laugh.

Then Calderon thought of something. "Sara, before you go, we need to talk."

Sara sobered a bit and walked back over. "What's up, Cal? Are you breaking up with me?" she said with her lips twitching and giving him sad eyes.

Calderon didn't smile, though. This has to be done, he thought sternly. Calderon began, "Kyle and I appreciate everything you have done for us and that you want to keep traveling with us."

"Uh, Calderon, what's going on? It's fine. We can trust her," said Kyle, perplexed.

Calderon continued somberly, "I do trust her, but we need to know everything, Sara. You said you left Eldall to find your father. Then, according to you, the troll took you, right?"

Sara nodded warily as she sat down next to Kyle. He moved closer to her, as though to protect her.

"Well, when we saved you, you suddenly wanted to leave the search for your father and everything behind. We need to know everything so we don't have something unforeseen come up," finished Calderon.

Sara sat looking at him sadly, her green eyes piercing Calderon's heart. He felt awful for broaching this now, but was there ever a good time?

Then Sara looked down and said, "I don't have anything to keep me in Eldall."

Then she pulled from her pocket the red piece of cloth Calderon had seen her with. Calderon now saw it was a red wool cap. "Before the troll took me, I found this . . . along with blood. It was . . . my father's," she said, a tear rolling down her round cheek.

Kyle put an arm around her and gave Calderon an angry look. Calderon cringed, feeling like he had done her a horrible wrong. All he could say was, "I'm so sorry, Sara. But I had to ask, and I could tell something was weighing on you."

She let out a shaky breath. "I appreciate it, Cal, and thank you for caring to ask. Before, I wanted to run off, run as fast as I could, run away from everything. Then, when you two found me and saved my life, I felt like, 'Wow, here's my purpose.' You know what I mean?"

Both Calderon and Kyle nodded. "You're always welcome with us, Sara. And you can always lean on us if you need to," said Kyle.

She smiled at them both, and Calderon felt the tension in the room fall away like it had never existed.

"Alrighty, then," Sara said, clapping her hands together once. "Enough of the sappy stuff. I'm gonna find King Landon, like I said." She hugged them both and hurried to the door. Looking back, she added simply, "Thank you, boys, for everything." Then she turned away, her blond braid swinging behind her as she hurried off.

Kyle lay back, lacing his hands behind his head, and took a deep breath.

Calderon and Kyle grinned.

"She really is something, isn't she?" said Calderon.

"She is. I'm glad we brought her with us," agreed Kyle.

"Did we have a choice?" said Calderon.

They both laughed, and Calderon went over and sat down on the bed next to his friend. Kyle sat up, rubbing at the back of his neck with one hand. Calderon wondered if Kyle's horns were causing his neck to hurt. Looking away, Calderon thought about mentioning to Kyle that maybe his horns were getting too big. However, he thought better of it because such a comment was insulting to some Kusarkus.

Suddenly, Calderon felt one of Kyle's long-fingered hands on his back in a comforting manner. Looking at Kyle, Calderon found his friend eyeing him with a worried, uncomfortable expression on his face.

"Listen, Cal. Like you just said to Sara, I want you to know I'm here if you need to talk," said Kyle.

Calderon looked at his friend and wondered what he could mean. "What do—" began Calderon, but Kyle cut him off.

"Just listen. I know what it's like. I killed that Dark Dwarf back at the start of our journey." Kyle looked away, his dark blue eyes distant, but Calderon didn't interrupt his friend's thoughts.

Continuing, Kyle said, "It bothered me for our whole journey. I mean, I took a life—even if it was necessary. And then I realized that was just it: it was necessary. But dealing with ending those lives we take is important. It means we don't ever take lives unless it is unavoidable for the protection of ourselves or others."

Calderon looked away, feeling his eyes water as he rubbed forcefully at them. Then he looked back at his friend, finding Kyle's eyes watery as well. Kyle cleared his throat, thumping Calderon's back.

"Thank you, Kyle. I'm sorry I didn't realize or think about how killing that dwarf would affect you," said Calderon.

Kyle's face brightened somewhat. "It's okay, Cal. I was trying to hide it well, anyway. Plus, you did me a favor." When Calderon raised an eyebrow, Kyle explained, "You brought me along. I could never have just sat around with my thoughts without doing something. Doing something helped me think more clearly," said Kyle.

Calderon nodded, thumping Kyle on the back in turn. "I appreciate it, Kyle. Listen, we will get through all this together, just like we started," Calderon assured him.

Kyle stood up, placing the plates and cups onto the tray. "I'll take care of this stuff. Just get some rest," said Kyle as he made his way to the door.

Calderon stood up, smiling warmly and opening the door for Kyle. "Thanks again, Kyle, for everything," said Calderon.

Kyle smiled at him and answered, "Of course. Any time, Cal."

Kyle left, and Calderon made his way to the bed and sat down on it, looking through his window at the rain, which was starting to pick up. Calderon lay back in his bed, listening to the rhythmic patter. It was nice that he had people like Kyle to talk to and lean on. He smiled, feeling like he wasn't as alone as he had felt.

"Kyle was right. I have to do my best. If I hadn't done what I did, bad things could have happened. I have responsibilities, both to myself and others," Calderon said quietly to himself. Relaxing fully, he fell asleep listening to the falling rain.

Calderon awoke suddenly. He wondered what could have happened. Could it be the storm outside that had picked up in intensity? Even now, he heard distant thunder. Then, a short, broad shadow moved quickly toward him. Calderon tried to roll away and off his bed, but the shadow was faster. The being caught him in a strong grip, covering Calderon's mouth with one callused hand.

"Easy, lad. It's just me," said a quiet, deep voice. Recognizing King Landon, Calderon's eyebrows crinkled in confusion. "That's right. I just didn't want you to wake up half the castle. Come on—me and the others need to talk to you in private. Just grab that sword of yours and follow me quietly."

Calderon, his mouth still covered, nodded, and Landon released him.

Rolling off his bed, he grabbed one of his tunics and hurriedly pulled it on. Locating his sword where he had left it by the window, he clasped the cuff to his left wrist and draped the chain over his shoulder. Then, tightening his sword belt, he turned to Landon.

The dwarf king was staring at him with a vacant expression,

apparently deep in thought.

"What's wrong?" asked Calderon in a hushed voice.

Landon shook his head, saying, "It's nothing, nothing at all. Only you really do look like him—Torin, I mean. But we should be going. Come on, lad, and keep quiet."

Surprised by the mention of his father, Calderon wondered if he did resemble Torin so much. Following Landon as quietly as possible, he made his way to a stairway and began to climb.

They continued up a tight spiral staircase Calderon surmised must be to one of the towers. The stairs, narrow on the inside curve and wider on the outside curve, had been made to be defended easily from people trying to climb the stairs and gain advantage of the towers. Passing one landing after another, they finally reached a shadowy platform with a small oak door. Calderon glanced at Landon, who nodded and opened the door, and Calderon walked inside.

The room was mostly dark, its only light showing on the opposite side, where Calderon saw all the leaders from the council gathering, except for Prince Elian, seated behind a table centered on a low dais. In the middle sat King Adam. To his right was Eryn. To his left, an empty seat, then Dragol, and next to him, Geshile. Landon moved past Calderon and took the empty chair.

As Calderon made his way to stand before the table, he saw four figures standing in the shadows, but he couldn't see who they were.

"Well, to what do I owe this pleasure? I thought we had said all that needed to be said at the last meeting. And where is Prince Elian?" asked Calderon in a pleasant tone, hoping to break the strong tension in the room.

To his relief, the leaders smiled in response. Then King Adam spoke. "We did say everything that needed to be said earlier about the other issues, but this is about you."

"Also, we believe Prince Elian is a traitor, which is why Neb is not here, either. He is keeping watch on the prince. We believe Elian had something to do with the attack on the Wizard High Council and the disappearance of his sister," said Eryn sadly.

Calderon quietly took that in, thinking he would have to tell Kyle he had been right. Still confused, Calderon looked up at the leaders of the Seven Kingdoms. "Have I done something wrong? Or is there something you would like me to do?" he asked.

The leaders looked at each other as though confirming something. Then, Eryn spoke up in his musical voice. "No, Calderon. We all have conferred and agree that it is time for you to lead your race as your father did."

Calderon put up his hands in a gesture of resistance. "Whoa! I'm no king, and I wasn't raised to be a king. By what right would I claim the throne after we gave up the right to rule ourselves to the elves?" argued Calderon, giving Eryn a grim nod.

It was King Adam who addressed the young Kusarku prince's concerns. "Calderon, you came to us for your training. We weren't training you to be just a soldier and merchant but to lead your race, to take your rightful place in your kingdom."

"Unlike most rulers, you have the support of the leaders of the other races, including the elves, though I'm sure Elian would disagree," added Dragol.

With a nod, Eryn concurred. "Both my king and the King of the Wood Elves stand with the son of Torin."

"But as I said, the Kusarkus will want to know why I deserve the throne. Some of them will not support me just because my father was king," argued Calderon, his voice rising. If he was honest with himself, he was nervous and a bit scared.

"If your people want proof of your right, they need look no further than the weapon you carry, son of Torin," said Geshile speaking up.

Calderon looked down at his sword, still puzzled. "My father's sword?" he asked softly. He wondered why that would be proof of him being worthy of being king.

Standing up suddenly and slamming a hand down on the table, King Landon exclaimed, "It's obvious, lad!" Then, continuing in a hushed voice, "The weapon you hold is one half of the Dragon's Tooth."

Calderon stood aghast and felt as though he might faint. He dazedly looked down at the weapon.

He drew the Dragon's Tooth and held it before him as though seeing it with new eyes. Even as he thought fleetingly that it was impossible to be true, things began clicking into place that should have been obvious. At once, he knew that it was, indeed, true and he had been blind. Thinking back, he remembered the looks he had gotten from Bard—excited and fearful looks. Also, it made sense now as to why it was not made of normal material, just as the old blacksmith had commented.

Looking up, apprehensive and for once not knowing what to say, he simply asked, "How?"

Eryn sat back in his seat and said, "I can explain . . . because I was with your father when we found the Dragon's Tooth." Calderon looked at the elf, wondering why he had never heard of this. Eryn continued, "Before the Grey War began, your father's kingdom was drifting apart. I was a good friend of your father's, along with Bard. Torin believed that through the magic of the sword, the Kusarku pride and loyalty could be stirred. I won't tell all, for it's a long story, save to say we found the sword deep in the Dark Woods, where there is a broken-down fortress."

King Adam cut in, adding, "At the time, I had been newly crowned King of the Humans and had read many accounts of an abandoned Kusarku fortress in the Dark Woods. Your father was very interested in the fortress and hurried to see what he could find there. Of course, the rest is obvious. He found the Dragon's Tooth, and even with its diminished strength, brought your people back together."

Geshile nodded and said, "But then, the Dark Elves invaded, and the Grey War began."

Calderon felt his mouth hanging open in his shock. Coming to himself, he asked, "But why didn't he keep looking for the rest of the sword?"

Eryn raised an eyebrow, "The war, as Queen Geshile said, and other things. One was the reformation of the kingdom. Another was his marriage to Queen Elaine. Soon, time was up, and he needed to make do with what he had. Also, we weren't sure, at the time, where the second piece was."

Calderon nodded in a daze. Then, with sudden shock, he grasped something Eryn had said. "At the time. Do you mean you know where it is now?"

King Adam nodded. "I have amassed countless manuscripts and many ancient tomes throughout my time both as a wizard and as king. I'm sure there is, within my library, one that can tell us where the weapon lies in wait."

Calderon nodded then asked, "So, what should I do?"

Dragol spoke up. "Find the second piece and carry on where your father left off."

Eryn added, "With the full power of the Dragon's Tooth, lead your people, for we fear these attacks have merely been a sign that a new war is brewing."

Then Landon, looking grave, cleared his throat. "And one more reason for having the sword again: we made need its power, for the wild dragons of the Fire Mountains are stirring once again."

Calderon felt pale and faint. He had wanted responsibility, but he suddenly felt as though he were holding back a storm. His eye caught a brief flash, and he looked down at the Dragon's Tooth. Suddenly, a flame awoke in his heart, and the sword glowed red-hot in answer. He would do this. For once, he knew his mission, his responsibility, his inheritance. His path was clear. Allowing his weapon's glow to fade, he sheathed it and looked back up at those seated at the table. They were all looking down at him, some with smiles, some with looks of concern.

"Your highness, you mentioned there could be writings that spoke of where I could find the second piece," said Calderon.

King Adam nodded. "Yes, I'm sure you will find it in my personal library. Your companions and Eryn will take you there."

Calderon turned at the sound of movement behind him as two of the figures from the shadows moved forward. It was Kyle and Sara. Both of them were smiling, and Calderon found himself smiling as well.

"You already agreed to us traveling with you, and you're not getting out of it," said Kyle with a wink.

Calderon smiled and said, "I wouldn't have it any other way."

Next, a third figure stepped into the light; it was Anna, who was blushing. King Adam cleared his throat, and Calderon looked back at him.

King Adam's eyes glimmered with amusement. "I hope it's not an imposition for one of my guards to go with you. I've heard that Anna, here, is seeking excitement in the outside world," he said.

"Of course, I would be honored to have her along," said Calderon with a smile and nod at Anna.

Calderon thought she could be useful. And how he could say no to King Adam?

Eryn then spoke up. "As most of the other races are represented in your party, I will be sending my own son with you as well."

Calderon turned to see Duncan step forward with a self-conscious smile. Duncan turned his head slightly and pulled his long brown hair back to show slightly pointed ears. Duncan was a half-elf.

Calderon thought back to their first meeting. "I thought you said your father died. And were you even hunting trolls when I met you?" asked Calderon, slightly hurt.

Duncan shook his head with a sad smile. Then he spoke, and his voice now had a slight musical tone. "I was sent by my father to look after you, in light of everything going on. We were concerned an enemy would discover you were the sole heir to the Kusarku throne. And, because the king is concerned about his son's . . . hot-headed disposition . . . we chose not to share the information with Prince Elian."

Calderon frowned, looking back over his shoulder at Eryn. Eryn smiled despite Calderon's expression. "Torin and Elaine would haunt me relentlessly from the Other Side if I allowed something to happen to their son."

Calderon gave him a nod of understanding and gazed back at Duncan—if that was even his name.

"It wasn't a complete lie," Duncan said, seeming to read Calderon's mind. "I was looking for a troll. But I was looking for you, also, and making sure the troll I'd heard of hadn't eaten Kusarku for dinner," continued Duncan with a conspiratorial smile.

"I understand," said Calderon stiffly, forgetting that he himself had been hiding his true identity for many years.

While Calderon understood why Duncan had done what he did, that didn't mean he had to like it. Also, it didn't mean Calderon had to trust Duncan, and he wouldn't until Duncan proved he could be trusted completely. Concerns about ethics and morals would have to wait for another day, though.

"You are all welcome, of course. I think I will need all the help I can get. And I would be a fool to not accept help wherever it's coming from," said Calderon, making deliberate eye contact with Duncan.

"Well, then, I think that is all good and settled," said Landon loudly.

Calderon turned back to the leaders, and his friends moved up to stand next to him.

"Thank you all for your confidence. I will do my best to live up to your expectations," said Calderon.

"See that you do, lad. I speak for both dwarf clans when I say we are more than ready to take back control of the mountains with the Kusarkus at our side," said Dragol, a smile lifting his beard.

Calderon smiled and nodded his agreement.

Just then, Kyle cleared his throat, and he flushed as everyone turned to look at him. "So, you were all saying we start with looking through these documents about the other piece of Cal's weapon."

Eryn nodded and stood up. "With King Adam's permission, I'll come with you to the library. As I was with Torin and helped him find the first piece of the Dragon's Tooth, I may be of help in finding something of importance more quickly," said Eryn.

King Adam stood as well and nodded with a fatherly smile. "Come see me when you have found what you're searching for," he said.

Calderon and his friends bowed to Queen Geshile and each of the kings, who returned the bows with nods of appreciation and dismissal. Turning, they then made their way to the door of the room, with Eryn hurrying to them in long strides so the six left the room together.

Chapter 16

Upon leaving the room, Eryn let out a whistle, and four elven guards came from the stairway, where they had been stationed. Calderon gave them a surreptitious look as they took up positions behind him and his companions. They wore dark leather, and each carried a longsword and shortsword on their back. Unlike Elian's guards, they wore no faceplates. All four were as tall and fair-skinned as Eryn, but the guards' hair was golden-blond rather than Eryn's dark brown shade.

Calderon glanced at Eryn and Duncan, who were walking together just in front of him as they went down the steps. Now that he looked at them next to one another, he could see the resemblance. Though Duncan had the rougher face of a human, there was something of Eryn about Duncan's eyes. Not only that, but they also moved with the same studied grace. Calderon couldn't help but feel angry about how they had lied to him. No matter the fact that they had done so to protect him. He felt like punching something or at least shouting at Duncan to make him feel some sort of remorse for his deception.

Coming back to himself as they reached the main floor, Calderon glanced to his right at Kyle, who was walking next to him. Kyle also was gazing at Eryn and Duncan with narrowed eyes. Noticing Calderon watching him, Kyle nodded as if to say, "I'll watch them both closely from now on." Instead, though, he said softly with a smirk, "I was right about Elian. You can't deny it."

Calderon, with a sheepish grin, answered, "Yes, you were. Now, let's see if we can use your great observation skills to find the information we need."

Kyle complained, "I hate reading; it always gives me a headache."

"Wait—you can read? Now I am impressed," teased Sara from behind them.

Anna giggled softly, and Calderon looked back at the two young women. Sara wore a dark tunic similar to the one they had met her in. Calderon could hear the tinkling of the chainmail she wore beneath it. Also, she carried a shortsword on her back and Kyle's dagger at her waist.

Anna, as ever, bore a lance and had a shortsword at her waist. However, today she had parted with her bright armor for well-worn dark green leather armor.

Both girls smiled at Calderon, and he quipped, "Just make sure Kyle does read and doesn't just pretend to look at the pages." They all laughed softly, and even Eryn and Duncan chuckled.

"Okay, okay. What type of clues are we looking for? I mean, do you think there will be a map that says, 'sword here' with a great big X marking the spot?" asked Kyle sarcastically.

"Hardly," Eryn said with a laugh. "It's more likely that there will be writings that mention something small or out of the ordinary. As I said before, when Torin and I found the first part of the sword, there had been only a mention of the building of a Kusarku fortress in the Dark Woods. And the Wood Elves who had investigated the outside of the fortress admitted to its existence."

"Well, let's hope it's in the library and not lost to time," said Anna softly.

Calderon glanced back at her, a question taking shape in his head. "Why you, Anna?" he asked abruptly. Anna blushed and Calderon went on hurriedly, "What I mean is, King Adam has hundreds of guards. Why out of all of his guards are you coming with us?"

Even as he asked, he remembered his first dinner with the king and the partial conversation he had overheard.

"It's because our king is insightful. He can see to the heart of a person, I guess," she said, shrugging.

Kyle looked back at her and asked, "What do you mean?"

Anna sighed wistfully. "I've never been content with living in the city. Living here all my life with brothers who were always doing great things while I was just left behind made me hungry for adventure. That's why I joined the guards in the first place. I thought I'd be happy doing that, but . . ." Anna's face fell.

Calderon and the others nodded in understanding. At one time or another, they had all felt the pull of adventure.

Anna looked up and smiled so suddenly it was like sunlight breaking through clouds. "King Adam is a great king; he knows his people. When he told me he was wanting me to go with you all, I jumped at the chance."

"I'm glad you did. I can't be the only girl on this journey," said Sara. The two giggled together, and Calderon smiled, happy to have a group like the one he did.

Looking sideways at Kyle, Calderon said softly, "I'm sorry I kept who I was from you. But . . . did you know somehow?"

Kyle met Calderon's eyes for a moment. "I put a few things together on my own, but I just kept it to myself. I figured if no one told me about it, then there must be a reason," answered Kyle.

The two friends smiled at each other, and Calderon was happy he still had Kyle by his side.

They rounded a corner and saw a large wooden door at the end of a hallway lit only by sparse torches. They had reached the lower levels of the castle. Along with their footsteps echoing off the bare stone walls, they heard the steady drip-drip of water onto the stone floor.

"I very much doubt that King Adam was mistaken about the existence of the volumes we need. Wouldn't you agree, Calderon?" asked Duncan.

Calderon nodded, saying, "I agree, and King Adam is not one to misplace or harm ancient tomes or scrolls once he has them in his possession."

Eryn pushed open the door and gave a mock bow to everyone behind him. Duncan grinned and stepped into the room with Calderon and the others following behind. The room was dark, but no water dripped there.

The room must be protected from anything that would hurt these manuscripts by some spell of King Adam's, Calderon thought.

"Can we get a light or something? I don't see any torches," said Kyle in an uneasy tone.

Calderon thought back to the spell he had used to shine lights into the thieves' eyes with Anna when he had summoned balls of light. Focusing on gathering light together, he released the spell. Ten balls of light glowed above his open palm. They were not very big, only the size of a fist, but they produced enough illumination to read by. Sending the spheres flying from him in a sweeping arm gesture, they flew to different parts of the room so no corner would be hidden in the shadows.

"Nice," said Kyle and Anna together, moving towards the mountainous shelves of books and scrolls.

"Oh, I don't know . . . I didn't mind the dark," said Sara ruefully.

Calderon chuckled, saying, "A dwarf always prefers a cave to a bright, sunny day."

"Light is always welcome. It lets me see your beauty all the easier," said Duncan smoothly.

Sara blushed and turned away while Kyle glowered at him and snorted like an angry boar. Duncan moved past them both and approached the old shelves, inspecting the books closely.

"How, exactly, are we supposed to find something in all these texts?" asked Anna, glancing at Calderon and Eryn.

Eryn answered her with a grin and said, "King Adam would never have a disorganized library. Also, it may help speed our search to look for works from the time of King Brutus, the last user of the Dragon's Tooth, or marked with King Brutus' name. When Torin and I searched years ago, that is where we found the information we sought."

They all gave Eryn quizzical looks. Without looking up from the book he was currently glancing through, Duncan answered, "The books seem to be organized in alphabetical order by subject."

"That will certainly speed things up, as long as Kyle knows what comes after A, B, C. Oh wait—Brutus starts with B. You'll be all right, Kyle," teased Sara. Sara was laughing so hard she leaned against Anna, who also laughed but looked a little uncertain, wondering if she was truly part of the group now.

Calderon and the others laughed as well. Even the elven guards gave a chuckle. Kyle scowled, though, and moved forward, reading the spines of the books with Duncan.

The rest of them followed suit, Sara still giggling softly. As Calderon inspected the books, he saw they were indeed in alphabetic order. The books and scrolls had a wide range in age. Some looked brand new while others looked like they predated the Kusarkus' arrival into the Seven Kingdoms.

Calderon walked along one bookcase, which seemed to contain subjects under the letter K, from knife-making to the Dwarf King Knob.

Then Duncan said loudly, "Over here! I found Brutus, but it might take a while to go through it."

Calderon and the others hurried over. Focusing on his spheres of light, Calderon moved them so they lit up the bookcase in question.

Soon, Calderon understood what Duncan had meant about it taking a while. Two shelves of books and scrolls were dedicated to King Brutus.

"Well, let's get started," said Kyle with a sigh as he grabbed a book at random.

They all followed his example. Calderon pulled out a book and found it to be about a vein of obsidian found in a dwarf mine. The dwarves had been reluctant to allow the Kusarkus to work on the vein. When a Kusarku mining group arrived, they were attacked by a dwarf contingent. This apparently led to both races mustering armies. To prevent a war, the Elf King Samson had brokered for peace.

Flipping through the pages more quickly, Calderon saw the remainder of the book was about the peace talks to develop rules regarding how the contested mine would be used. Putting down that book, Calderon looked up to see the rest of the group searching persistently.

Eryn was reading an old scroll, his eyes flicking down the page.

Sara sat, legs crossed, with a small book in her lap. Anna leaned against a wall, a book in one hand and one of Calderon's lights bobbing over her shoulder. Kyle and Duncan were poring over a large book. Kyle had his eyes narrowed in concentration, while Duncan read over Kyle's shoulder with a humorous expression on his face.

Calderon picked up another scroll but put it down again quickly; it was a poem on the morning glory. He didn't have time to think wistfully about a vine. Why would that be here in King Brutus' section? wondered Calderon as he pulled out another book.

This one was certainly interesting, and Calderon found himself spellbound by its contents. There had been a dragon attack on the Kusarku city of Nighthall. King Brutus himself had gone to aid Nighthall with the Dragon's Tooth at his side. Amazed, Calderon took in all he could about how King Brutus, with the help of a dragonrider, had slain the great red dragon Cinder.

The dragonrider had flown King Brutus over Cinder as the dragon attacked a contingent of lancers. Brutus had landed on Cinder's back, and before he could react, Brutus had wrapped the chain of the Dragon's Tooth around the creature's neck.

Calderon found the rest of the page written in Brutus' own words:

Once I had the chain in place through the blessings of the great flame, Flagrash, I heated it. This burned into Cinder's ventral neck scales, which were cool. This, according to my father, causes no pain to the dragon but gives you a type of rein to keep yourself from being dislodged. Putting all of Flagrash's power into the Dragon's Tooth, I plunged it into the worm's neck. I thank the Great Flagrash for his power and sent this usurper to meet its maker.

Calderon found himself breathless and giddy. This weapon was now his. He could write his own tale of the Dragon's Tooth, too, one day and be held in awe by his own descendants . . . if, he thought soberly, he could live through his present and future struggles.

Suddenly, there came a loud clearing of someone's throat, and Calderon looked up. Kyle and Duncan were holding a scroll and looking pleased with themselves. Calderon thought Kyle looked like a self-satisfied cat that had just caught a mouse.

"I believe I have found something. Wouldn't you agree, Duncan?" said Kyle in a mock-snobbish voice but with a look of merriment in his eyes.

"I would concur with your observation, my good man," said Duncan in an equally haughty tone and straightening his tunic as though it were the most elegant court attire.

Calderon laughed, saying, "Let's see it, then," as he hurried over to them.

The others crowded around as well and looked at the old, weathered manuscript.

"I don't see what's so important about this," said Sara, giving Kyle and Duncan a quizzical look.

Calderon couldn't help but agree with her. The manuscript appeared to be an itemized listing of supplies—from tools and firewood to food stores and medicinal herbs—for a settlement. Included also were the plans for a small stronghold built into a cliffside.

"It's not what's on the list that is important but the location," said Duncan, pointing to a line towards the top of the manuscript. Kyle unrolled the bottom of the scroll to show a small map of the Fairy Woods. And some distance east of the elven city of Hawthorne at the edge of the Fairy Woods was a small red X.

Calderon stared at the map, his mouth agape. "I hadn't thought we would actually find something so pointed," said Calderon quietly. The Fairy Woods. Just thinking of all the wild magic and unexplained creatures rumored to live there gave Calderon a shudder. From somewhere in the distance, Calderon heard and felt the boom of thunder from the increasing storm. Anna looked up at the ceiling of the library, her brow furrowed.

"Of course we found it. Never doubt King Adam—a lesson for you all. Also, would it make sense to hide the Dragon's Tooth, to have it never be found rather than simply put away for safekeeping? King Brutus was a crafty one," said Eryn, beaming. The excitement in his eyes made him look as young as Duncan.

"Shouldn't we continue to look to see if we can find more mention of this place?" asked Sara, pulling out another book and sitting back down with her legs crossed.

"I agree. Maybe there is more information we may need in the future," said Calderon. Following her lead, he grabbed another scroll from the bookcase. The others, too, went back to their research just as a louder boom of thunder rattled the bookcases.

As they read, the storm seemed to bloom around the castle. After what seemed an indeterminate amount of time but was closer to twenty minutes, Sara let out a squeal. "Ah! What's this? Everyone! Come look!" she exclaimed, nearly shouting.

They all hurried over to find Sara holding a small, folded piece of paper.

"It was between the pages of this book. It talks about the peace talks that took place regarding the Kusarkus giving up the Dragon's Tooth," said Sara excitedly.

"Well, open it. What does it say, shorty?" said Anna, hopping from foot to foot.

Sara stuck her tongue out at Anna and opened the paper. Sara cleared her throat and read, "'Flowing like water, let fire flow like lava. Sword become tool, and weapon be tooth.' What do you think that means? It must be something about your weapon, Cal, but what?"

Shrugs went around the room like a wave.

"I don't know, but let's hold on to both pieces of paper," said Calderon. Turning, he saw Eryn looking at him with his eyes bright and a big smile on his face.

"Well, let's get you all to King Adam and show him what we have found," said Eryn.

They were all nodding in agreement when another huge thunderclap boomed, but this time it sounded like the castle itself had broken. Now silent, they looked up at the ceiling and walls as if in fear that they might crumble on top of the group. Then, Calderon heard very distinctly the clip-clopping of hooves in the hallway outside, coming their way.

They all looked at one another. The elven guards, who had been standing at ease at the door, moved to a position in front of Calderon and his companions. Suddenly, the room felt like a prison and the air around them became stale. Anna held her lance in a ready position, her eyebrows pulled together in one severe line. Eryn and Duncan stepped forward to stand with the guards as the hoofbeats, and also now many other footsteps, could be heard.

The storm battering the castle walls now seemed of little importance. All that mattered now was who was approaching the king's private library in such a large number in the middle of the night. Then, with the suddenness of a lighting flash, the hallway fell silent.

Elian suddenly leapt around the corner and into the open doorway like a magician revealing a trick. He wore gold scale armor that fit him well. An ornate longsword hung at his side and looked like a piece of art. His blond hair fell in a cascade to his shoulders. Elian seemed a different person, now, as he positively bounced on his toes then said with apparent joy, "Hello, hello! I'm so happy to find you all here and together. Especially you, Eryn. Finally, we can deal with all the elven issues in one stroke. You know, all the rats in one trap."

Indeed, as he finished, he laughed so hard his armor clinked, and Calderon couldn't help but hear what sounded like madness in the elven prince's cackling.

Calderon shifted uncomfortably. Something was wrong here; this was definitely a trap—but why? As Kyle nudged him, giving Calderon a look that said, "I told you so," Calderon happened to see his own sword. His mind jumped; whoever was after them all was after the Dragon's Tooth.

Chapter 17

"So, Elian, you show your true colors, a traitor to your own kind and even your father," said Eryn softly.

Elian's eyes narrowed with anger, and his smile turned into a clench-toothed grimace. Suddenly, with all decorum gone, he roared, "I am no traitor. I simply take measures others wouldn't dare. Enough sniveling and groveling to the other races. The Seven Kingdoms? Pah!" and he spat on the ground. Mastering himself slowly, he continued, his voice shaking with emotion, "When my designs are complete, there will be one kingdom that rules, and that will be the elves. How is that the work of a traitor? I ask you, Eryn."

"And what would you have happen to the rest of the races, like mine?" asked Calderon, trying to control his anger and disbelief.

Elian laughed, saying, "You can leave this land or bend your knee to the true rulers."

Eryn then said quietly, "Where is your sister? What have you done?"

Elian raised his hands as though he bore no blame. "I did what I had to. She's still alive, of course. I wouldn't kill my own sister—even if she is a misguided fool like the rest of you."

Duncan stepped forward cautiously, as though Elian were a wild animal. "Would you give up everything our race has strived to build?" Duncan asked.

"Don't speak to me as if we are kin, half-breed," spat Elian. He turned his gaze on Eryn and said, "And you reproach me as a traitor to my kind while you sire your own half-breed?

"We've had enough talk time," exclaimed Elian, "for the rat trap to snap shut!"

He drew his sword with a flourish while four elven guards, wearing helmets and full faceplates, rushed into the room. After them came goblins armed with their crude swords and axes. Then, over the clamor of the enemy, came slow hoofbeats.

Calderon drew his sword at last, and next to him, he heard the groan of Kyle's bowstring being pulled back. Into the room came a huge Kusarku more than a head taller than Kyle and built like a sculpture of the pinnacle of man.

Calderon felt his muscles tense. He had seen this Kusarku before. His red eyes had blazed from the darkness of a cave in a dream. The huge Kusarku wore no armor, only knee-length leather leggings over his charcoal-colored skin. Over one heavily muscled shoulder could be seen the blade of a massive battle-ax. His horns were enormous. He looked more like a real minotaur than a Kusarku.

"May I introduce a friend of your father's, little prince. This is General Krasp," exclaimed Elian with evident delight.

White-hot anger leapt up in Calderon, and he made to jump forward and attack. However, he felt someone grab his shoulder, holding him back.

Calderon screamed anyway, "Traitor, how dare you side with enemies of your own people!"

He made to shake off whoever was holding him, but they had a firm grip. Hot tears of anger and frustration ran down Calderon's face. Then Krasp roared with laughter so thunderous it rang around the room and drowned out all other sounds.

"So, you're Torin's whelp," snorted Krasp, his voice deep and rough. "You call me a traitor? With every new generation, the royals of our people look more and more human! At least Bard the half-breed has horns—unlike you."

Calderon found himself shaking with anger; he could stand abuse thrown at himself but not at Bard or his parents. "Bard and my parents are three times the Kusarku you are, traitor!" screamed Calderon. Krasp laughed, as did Elian, his guards, and the goblins. The dark cacophony filled the air.

Calderon heard his friends moving behind him. Leather armor creaked as they moved and adjusted their grips on weapons. Repositioning his own weapon, Calderon began concentrating his imposing will to draw the magical heat of the Dragon's Tooth for battle. If the enemy noticed, they didn't seem to care.

Raising a delicate hand to his mouth, Elian attempted to stifle his laughter with apparent difficulty and announced, "All of you, surrender for your own good. There is no need for all of you to die.".

When none of them moved to heed his command, Elian sighed and raised his hand in a "Don't blame me, then" gesture. He signaled Krasp and ordered, "Kill them all."

The tension in the room felt like a tangible object. Calderon, still shaking with rage, suddenly realized they all might die there among the old scrolls and books, with their blood stains the only evidence of Elian's and Krasp's crimes.

I have to protect my friends, thought Calderon. As if in answer, the Dragon's Tooth glowed redder, and Calderon's spheres of light seemed to grow brighter.

Krasp grinned with joyous anticipation and drew his monstrous battle-ax. Raising the ax over his head, he roared and gestured for the attack. The goblins yelled and screamed and leapt towards Calderon and his friends.

Calderon sent his balls of light flying at the goblins, trying to make them flinch.

It worked. The goblins, so used to dark places, tried to cover their hideous green faces with their long-fingered hands. An arrow suddenly flew past Calderon's ear and buried itself in the neck of one of the distracted creatures. He next saw Anna leap forward with her lance, driving the point into yet another goblin with a sickening crunch.

"Watch out!" yelled Duncan.

Calderon and his friends hit the ground as though they had fainted. The goblins howled, ready to kill the enemies at their feet. Then, with a creak of old wood and a flurry of falling books, a bookshelf smashed into more goblins and then flew through the air, hitting two of the elves that stood next to Elian. Elian, however, leapt away like a cat.

"Now, Eryn, what would the king say about destroying all these old books?" chortled Elian.

Calderon and his friends got to their feet and hooves. Shooting Eryn a look of approval, he began to swing the Dragon's Tooth, circling the blade so it was a glowing red ring in the air.

The goblins and elves charged. Calderon, Anna, Sara, and Duncan, along with Eryn's elven guards, ran forward to meet them. Another arrow from Kyle flew through the air to hit an enemy elf in the leg. At the last moment, Sara slid on her back and cut the legs out from under another goblin. Duncan smashed a goblin in the head with his ax as the creature tried to grab Sara.

A storm of books pelted two more of the elves in front of Calderon. Swinging his sword in an upward cut, he sliced through one elf's torso. As the sword reached its pinnacle, Calderon pulled down on the chain. The sword cut diagonally in the opposite direction on the second elf, felling him.

A goblin with an immense, bulbous nose ran at Calderon with its sword raised. Drawing back his arm, Calderon threw the Dragon's Tooth. It hit the goblin in the sternum, and he went down with a strangled cry. Breathing hard with a surge of adrenaline, Calderon pulled his weapon free and looked up. Krasp stood feet from him with a cruel grin on his face.

"Come on, little prince. Let's see if you're truly worthy of your name," Krasp growled. Two of Eryn's elven guards lay at his feet, one with a huge gash in his head. The other one was missing his left arm and still screaming in pain. Blood dripped from Krasp's ax and horns.

To Calderon, the screams of the dying seemed muffled as he focused on the giant before him. "Surrender, Krasp. I am the rightful heir to the

Kusarku throne. Surrender and face your fate with honor," said Calderon in a level tone.

Krasp leered at him, saying, "I think our people are done with the old ways of succession. Only the strong should rule." And lifting his ax, Krasp beckoned Calderon forward.

Without hesitation, Calderon rushed toward him and swung his weapon as fast as he could, aiming to cut down his enemy in a single attack. The Dragon's Tooth glowed red-hot, and Calderon knew Krasp would die.

Krasp, though, leaned back like a young tree swaying in the wind. Without pausing, Calderon swung again, this time letting go of the Dragon's Tooth, hoping that with more reach, Krasp wouldn't be able to evade him. But Krasp swung his ax with lightning speed and smacked the Dragon's Tooth aside by hitting the flat of the blade.

Calderon blinked in surprise, and Krasp gave him a toothy grin. "Come on, kid. I knew your father. You don't have anything that will surprise me."

Calderon was starting to lose his focus on the Dragon's Tooth, and it had begun to cool. He growled, pulling on his weapon and turning in a circle. With his hand clasped tight on it, he attempted to wrap the chain around Krasp's legs. Calderon felt the cuff dig into his wrist as he swung the chain, but he ignored the pain. Krasp jumped over the chain as if he were playing jump rope. He came down in front of Calderon and punched him hard in the mouth. Tasting blood, Calderon fell onto his back, his face feeling like it had been hit by a hammer.

Calderon opened his eyes in time to see Krasp above him raising his ax to strike. Kicking upward as hard as he could, Calderon caught Krasp in the left knee. Gritting his teeth, Krasp stepped back, hobbling. Spinning onto his hooves, Calderon rushed at Krasp, swinging the Dragon's Tooth at the general's injured right side. Krasp's ax knocked the Dragon's Tooth aside again, and Calderon nearly lost his grip on it. Calderon's weapon was now flickering hot then cold and back again. Sweat beaded the young Kusarku's face with the effort he brought forth to concentrate on the Dragon's Tooth.

Though it had taken only a moment, Krasp was already moving

forward to take advantage of Calderon's loss of attention in the fight. Krasp was nearly to him when Calderon had an idea. He swung the sword again, but this time with the chain linked in his right hand.

Just like the times before, Krasp was faster and evaded the blade. But as the sword was knocked aside, Calderon threw the blistering-hot chain into Krasp's face. Grabbing his seared visage and screaming in fury, Krasp stepped back quickly. Calderon rushed forward, and with the scorching Dragon's Tooth, he swung at Krasp's left shoulder. Krasp's eyes grew wide as he tried to get his ax up and around, but he was too late. Just as the blade was about to slice into his shoulder, Krasp leaned back so fast he nearly fell. The hot blade still gave a shallow cut. However, even though it was glancing blow, the skin around the cut turned black. The wound, of course, wasn't life-threatening, but at least Calderon had scored a hit.

"Bastard," screamed Krasp, and he kicked Calderon hard in the stomach.

All the wind went out of Calderon, and he went down hard on his face. He couldn't catch his breath; it felt like a huge weight was sitting on his chest. Had he broken a rib? He had to get some air into his lungs. Krasp was going to kill him if he didn't get up. He tried again to take a breath, but it still wouldn't come. Calderon gasped and sputtered then, to his relief, he breathed a small, ragged breath and then, with difficulty, a second.

From what sounded like a long way off, he heard someone yell, "Let's get out of here! We've done all we can." Looking up, he saw Krasp and Elian hurrying from the room. Krasp held his shoulder tightly with one hand, and the flesh around his hate-filled right eye was charred where the chain had struck him. Calderon saw the general's other hand was held to his belly near where an arrow shaft protruded. Another arrow from Kyle struck the doorway just as Krasp and Elian disappeared.

It registered with Calderon, then, what had happened. Kyle must have shot Krasp, yet again saving Calderon's life.

Calderon looked back at his friends, relieved to see they were okay. Anna had a bloody lip, and Sara was covering a long, shallow cut in her left arm. Duncan was limping, but Calderon couldn't see any blood, although he could see blood on his weapons. Elian seemed unhurt, but he was leaning on a broken bookshelf, breathing hard. Kyle, of all of them, hadn't gotten a scratch, being in the back. Of the four elven guards who had accompanied them, two were left, though bruised and moving gingerly, which was saying something for an elf.

The room, however, was in worse shape. Books and scrolls were scattered around it like a storm had thrown them about. Three bookshelves were in ruins, and Calderon winced inwardly thinking of how upset King Adam might be at the destruction of his library and the fathoms of history held here. Then, a larger boom than ever shook the castle, bringing Calderon back to his senses.

"We have to go after them," he rasped while struggling to his feet; his ribs hurt badly. Kyle hurried forward, helping Calderon to stand.

"He's right. We have to capture those two—they may have information we need," said Eryn, standing up straight.

"Heck yeah, let's get those bastards," said Sara, making Calderon smile in spite of his soreness.

Calderon hurried from the room with his friends close behind. The hallway was just as before, except for the scarlet droplets on the floor. Against one wall was a red smear where someone had leaned against it. A few feet further was a spatter of blood on the floor along with Kyle's arrow, now broken and useless. Calderon was starting to feel anxious, and his back tensed.

What if the enemy has already gotten away? What if I was too slow? thought Calderon furiously. Had he let down all the leaders who had believed in him?

"At least we hurt them, and they didn't get their way. That has to count for something," said Kyle from behind him as though he had read Calderon's thoughts.

Calderon couldn't agree with him. I got batted around like I was a child. It was just a lucky shot and a flesh wound that put Krasp on the defensive at all. I must do better and prove that the faith others have in me wasn't wrong, Calderon silently berated himself.

"Why were those elves fighting alongside him?" asked Anna. "I can understand a couple being traitors, like the ones from the meeting, but how many elves has he turned to his side?"

Duncan sighed and shrugged. Eryn blew out a breath slowly and then said quietly, "I don't know. Before today, I would have said it was rare indeed for an elf to betray their people, but tonight's events fly in the face of that."

At last, they reached the stairs, and without pausing, everyone hurried up them with Calderon in the lead. As they climbed, Calderon began to hear new sounds above the clatter of their footsteps: cries of pain, steel clashing against steel, and of people fighting. Maybe some guards had caught Krasp and Elian and were fighting them. Perhaps Calderon would catch them after all.

Excitement and trepidation rushed through him, and he put on a burst of speed. His chest heaved and his ribs burned so much that his eyes stung with tears, but he kept going. Kyle was just behind him.

They burst into the wide hall and stood, thunderstruck, at the sight that met them. The far wall had been blasted inward. From within the avalanche of rock could be seen twisted limbs of people who had been vibrant and alive but a short time before. Dust still clung in the air along with smoke from smoldering fires where rugs and tapestries burned. The scent of blood and smoke was strong. Calderon tasted copper on his tongue. He saw, without being surprised by it, the blast marks of what was unmistakably spellwork. Calderon wondered where the spellcasters were now.

A few guards fought a couple of goblins trying to reach the far stairs. These goblins were all that remained inside, but they fought with a ferocity that was gruesome to behold. Calderon spat; his mouth felt like it was coated with the dust in the air. He wiped his face with the back of his hand and felt grit and what was likely sweat.

Suddenly, Sara jumped forward and pointed with her shortsword. By the breach in the wall, Krasp and Elian were climbing over the debris. Krasp barked something at the goblins and then hurried over the fallen chunks of stone.

Calderon started across the hall with his friends at his back. Out of the corner of his eye, he caught movement and saw it was Kon and John. Sir John was sitting, his legs sprawled in front of him. There was a large rent in his golden armor, and blood flowed freely from it. Sir Kon was on one knee, trying his best to stanch the bleeding while yelling at his guards and for a healer at the same time. The guards were milling about, and Calderon saw confusion and loss in their eyes.

Calderon looked back at his enemies and the hole in the wall. Krasp was yelling something at goblins outside the hole as he hurried off with Elian in tow. The goblins outside were starting to form into a group to attack. Calderon ground his teeth as Krasp and Elian were getting away.

What was he supposed to do? Should I help Sir John? I want to, but then what about the goblins? And for that matter, what about everyone else who is left? These thoughts fought for control, pulling him in all directions.

"What do we do, Calderon? We have to do something," said Anna, breaking into his thoughts.

Calderon looked back at her. Her eyes were full of tears, but she held her weapons ready. Calderon realized they were looking to him to lead them. Calderon found this information galvanizing. This was his opportunity to prove himself.

Calderon turned to his friends and spoke as clearly and confidently as his shaking voice would let him. "Eryn, do you know any healing spells or anything that could help the injured?" Eryn nodded and Calderon pointed to John. "Do what you can for John and the others who need the most attention." Eryn hurried away while Calderon watched him go, hoping John would be okay.

Then Calderon continued, "You two"—he pointed to the elf guards—"help the guards mop up the last of the goblins inside. Then gather the soldiers for a counterattack." The elves nodded wordlessly and moved off, drawing their swords.

Calderon turned back to his friends, taking a deep breath even though it hurt. "The rest of us are going to hold the castle till reinforcements come . . . if they can," said Calderon.

Duncan frowned and asked, "But what about Krasp and Elian? We can't just let them go."

Calderon shook his head. "We have to do what we can here and let the future make up its own mind on the outcome."

Kyle let out a short laugh. "Okay, Cal. You've obviously got a plan, so let's hear it."

Calderon drew his weapon and began walking toward the breach. Already, goblins were milling outside, gathering in number, ready to overrun the castle any minute.

Calderon pointed ahead of him, saying, "We should use the pile of rocks to our advantage. Make the enemy come to us. They will be slow and make our job all the easier." Then he said in a louder voice, "Until reinforcements arrive, guard each other's backs, and we will all make it out of this. Kyle, bring down as many as you can before they reach us."

Kyle nodded. The others looked nervous but had their weapons ready. As they reached the edge of the wall debris, Calderon and his friends fanned out in a line. The hole was only seven feet across, so only so many goblins could come through at one time.

As they waited there, Sir Kon ran up to Calderon, his heavy footfalls thudding loudly even over the sounds of small skirmishes still going on inside and the goblins amassing outside. Calderon half turned to him along with Anna, who brought her fist to her chest in a quick salute. Kon returned the salute hurriedly and turned his attention to Calderon and the goblins preparing to charge.

From behind Kon, a blue light emanated from Eryn's hands as he held them over John, casting his healing spells. Calderon couldn't see John's injury from where he stood; he just hoped Eryn's spells were having an effect.

I can't lose Sir John. I don't want to lose anyone, thought Calderon sadly.

Turning to Sir Kon, Calderon met his sad and worried eyes. "Calderon, you and the others have to flee. The goblins have separated our forces here at the castle from those manning the walls. We can't regroup here. We have to fall back."

Calderon shook his head and turned back to the now-approaching goblins. They were fifty yards away and moving toward them in a steady march, as if daring the castle defenders to attack.

"We will hold them here so you can gather your men. Use dragons or something to get the two groups to act as one," argued Calderon.

Sir Kon shook his head and said, "Dragons are no good to us in this storm, and most of our dragons here are small."

Calderon nodded; he should have thought of that. The deluge of rain was so hard he wondered if even big dragons could fly through it. It didn't matter, though. Calderon had chosen his path—to stand there, defending the castle alongside his friends. Then he turned to Kon and barked, "Gather your men for a counterattack. Until then, we will hold the line. Now go!"

Kon smiled in spite of everything and gave Calderon a nod. Running off, the Leader of the Guard drew his huge sword and attacked the remaining goblins in the hall, furiously barking orders the whole time at his men.

Calderon smiled at his friends, and they smiled back. Beginning to swing his sword on its chain in short circles, he focused on the enemy.

The goblins had reached the breach in the wall and heedlessly began to hobble over the debris. There was a twang from Kyle's bow, and one goblin went down to be stepped on by his comrades.

Calderon waited to call upon the magic in his sword; he had learned from his battle with Krasp that it was hard to focus his will while fighting for long periods of time. Therefore, he would use the sword's power when he needed it. Now was not a time to get tired out from seeing how far he could push his will. He knew that, with time and practice, his endurance would get better, but now was not the time to experiment.

A second goblin went down with an arrow in its gut. Calderon saw another, this one fatter, stumble over some stone only feet away. Spinning the chain faster in quick rotation to increase momentum, Calderon threw the Dragon's Tooth. It stuck deep in the goblin's belly, making him gasp and fall forward as Calderon pulled the blade free.

Anna stabbed forward, catching another goblin in the leg and, when he stumbled, in the chest. Simultaneously, Calderon, concentrating on his magic, raised a large rock and sent it flying at the goblins. The rock hit one in front of Sara, and she ended its struggles to rise from the ground with a sturdy thrust of her shortsword.

Duncan was a marvel to behold as he blocked a goblin's sloppy blow with his sword. He then swung his short battle-ax up and around to split the creature's skull. Next, he did it again like he had practiced the move over and over.

Kyle continued to steadily fire, diminishing the goblins' numbers and making them easier to fight. Focusing his will for a moment, Calderon brought the heat from the depths of the Dragon's Tooth. Then, as two goblins approached, he cut through their swords as they attacked him from either side. As the goblins stared in horror at their useless weapons, Calderon dispatched them both with two quick thrusts. The bodies of the fallen goblins began to add to the pile of debris, making it even more difficult to navigate.

Calderon dueled a long-limbed goblin, blocking and thrusting and parrying until he caught the goblin in the hip. The creature stumbled, and Calderon ended him. From beside him, Anna shouted and threw her lance, catching a goblin in the ribs with a crunch. Sara, taking a cue from Calderon, began to throw fist-sized stones at the screeching, cursing goblins. The air smelled of burned flesh, a sickly sweet odor. Along with that came the stench of the goblins' blood, which smelled oddly like sulfur. Calderon breathed it in while trying to ignore the miasma and remain focused.

Two goblins were holding each other up while making their way over the rubble. Concentrating on his magic and gathering the electricity around him, Calderon shot a bolt of electricity at them. They screamed and fell on the stones, their flesh smoking slightly.

Calderon shot a second bolt at a goblin that was quickly jumping over the stones like a mountain goat. He fell with a croak of pain. Turning from that dying goblin, Calderon, not a moment too soon, blocked a brutal swing at his legs from another that had crept up to him. Focusing again on his will, Calderon knocked the goblin's blade aside and then threw the hot chain up and over the goblin's head. As Calderon yanked it back, the hot chain sent the goblin sprawling to the ground. Calderon stabbed downward and quickly cut short its screeching.

Glancing quickly around, Calderon was in awe of his friends, who were holding their own, but he wondered how long they could hang on.

Even as he thought this, a thicket of arrows flew from behind him, sending ten goblins down to those already dead or dying. Then there were men with lances and spears at his right and left. The lancers thrust and took down one goblin after another. With more men gathering, Calderon yelled for another volley of arrows. His call was answered, and more goblins went down to meet their brothers.

Sir Kon was next to Calderon now. He shouted, "Push them back. Archers, give our spearmen room to move."

The spearmen began to scramble over the hill of stones and bodies. Calderon and his friends joined them—all except for Kyle, who kept up his steady stream of arrows. The bodies were squishy, and Calderon had to watch his step across the slippery, blood-soaked stones. Trying not to think about it or how many he had killed, Calderon steadily made his way into the rain. It was cold, and soon he and his comrades were all drenched. Calderon brought forth the Dragon's Tooth's magic, and it steamed as rain hit the hot surface.

Before him was the wide area of the marketplace. A few goblins fled into the alleys, but the rest ran at the defenders. Calderon focused as hard as he could on his sword, readying himself for the goblins' charge. This fight was different with no rubble to trip over. Calderon began cutting and slashing as quickly as he could, trying to not give the goblins a moment to attack. Instead, he took the fight to them, cutting through sword, ax, and goblin, one after another.

Over the clamor of the fight, Calderon could hear the sounds of the people of Alezadria. People screamed with fear and pain. Somewhere, a baby was crying. He had to keep the fight contained to protect them.

Every now and then, Calderon would catch glimpses of his friends as they fought through the storm of rain and goblins. Calderon's shoulder soon began to ache, and he was breathing hard. He couldn't maintain his concentration on heating his blade. Water ran into his eyes, and Calderon wiped it away. As he did so, a goblin tackled him and growled menacingly in his ear. Calderon felt a stab of pain in his hip and drove his hooves into the goblin, kicking it off him. The goblin landed next to Calderon with a gasp, and Calderon stabbed it with two quick thrusts.

Calderon rose in pain and looked down at his side where a small dagger protruded from his hip. His blood was hot as it ran down his leg. Seeing Calderon was injured, a second goblin ran at him. Knowing he would die otherwise, Calderon focused with all his might, and his sword once again glowed red. With relief, Calderon easily cut through the goblin's ax and then the goblin itself. Its disembodied head hit the ground with a splat.

There was a shout from someone behind Calderon and then the unmistakable roar of a dragon. The blue dragon from before charged into the screaming goblins with its rider on its back stabbing and slashing at any goblin that got close enough. A jet of fire shot from the dragon's mouth, and more goblins fell. Suddenly, the dragon turned its sharp eyes on Calderon. He felt like it was waiting for orders or something, but the dragon's eyes narrowed, and it swung at him with long claws like spear tips.

Ducking and bewildered, Calderon was suddenly afraid as he fell to the ground, his ribs flaring painfully. However, the claws swept past him to cut down a goblin that had been right behind Calderon. Calderon rolled to his hooves with a groan.

"You all right?" yelled Kara the dragonrider.

Grinning, Calderon nodded his thanks to her and the dragon. The blue dragon, to Calderon's surprise, nuzzled him gently as it walked past. Looking up at the dragon, Calderon whispered to it, his hand on its scaly cheek, "Now, burn up those goblins."

He didn't expect anything, but to his surprise, the dragon lowered his head in acknowledgement. Turning, Calderon pointed at some goblins that were gathering in a group to attack. "Get them," he shouted even though it hurt.

The dragon roared its challenge, charging through the rain. The rain ran down its sides, making the dragon look sleek and deadly. Turning its head from one side to the other, the dragon raked the goblins with fire.

In that spare moment, Calderon pulled the dagger blade from his hip. He screamed with pain, and blood pulsed from the now-open wound.

Bringing to mind what he knew of healing, Calderon focused on bringing first his flesh then skin back together. The bleeding stopped, but Calderon knew he had only lightly healed the wound. Any quick or hard movements could open the cut back up again. Luckily, he knew it wasn't life-threatening, but he'd had to remove the dagger because he couldn't move well with it in. Testing his weight on his leg, Calderon made his way back into the fray.

Now that a wedge had been forced into the goblin ranks, the fight was turning into a rout. Many goblins began to turn and flee. Calderon focused on the battle. A big goblin cut down the man next to Calderon, and Calderon punched the goblin hard in the gut. The goblin only grunted and swung at Calderon in return. The Kusarku prince dodged under the blow and stabbed the goblin, which fell back with a gurgling exhalation as the wind left its lungs.

There was a formidable yell of challenge from behind Calderon. It was the two dwarf kings and Geshile leading their warriors to the fight. The dwarves and Sobex warriors slammed into the enemy's left flank. The dwarves hacked and slashed their way into goblins, while the Sobex slashed with long scimitars or bit into the goblins, crushing bone and flesh, with their huge jaws.

Suddenly, the goblins were all turning and running. Calderon looked around and saw men pouring in from the alleys in the direction of the wall. The reinforcements had arrived. Calderon smiled, knowing this would ensure their victory. They had done it! Then Anna and Sara were around him and began helping him walk back to the castle.

"Are you all right, Cal? I saw you take that hit," said Sara with a worried look up at him.

Calderon tried to smile, but now that the battle was over, he realized he was aching all over and felt worse than ever. "I'll be okay. Nothing that some sleep and food can't fix," he answered.

They were all covered with blood and grime. He was happy to see that none of his group appeared to be seriously injured.

Then Anna shook him slightly, saying in a distraught voice, "Calderon, what about King Adam? Where has he been in all this?"

Calderon felt cold fear rush through him and said, "I don't know, but we'll find him."

They began to walk as quickly as Calderon's injury would allow back to the great hall. As they did, Kyle and Duncan hurried up to them.

"We've got to go check on the king. Let's check the throne room first," said Calderon hastily.

As a group, the six of them entered the hall. Calderon noticed Duncan's arm was bleeding from a long cut across his triceps. Apparently, Duncan didn't notice it as he hurried with them across the body-strewn hall and up the stairway.

At the top of the stairs, there appeared to be only a few dead goblins, which Calderon hoped was a good sign. Kyle took over for Anna, helping Calderon as he limped on his bad hip. Anna hurried to the throne room doors and threw one open. They all hurried inside and stood in the doorway, shocked. On the floor were five blackened, smoking forms, and leaning against his staff, bent and breathing hard, was King Adam.

The room around him was torn apart, the windows were shattered, and rain splashed into the room. The throne was broken and turned on its side. All the walls of the room bore scorch marks from spell blasts. So severe was the destruction that Calderon could see cracks in the walls and floors. Tiles had been ripped from the floor and thrown to shatter around the room.

Anna rushed over to the king, and as she did, he took a sigh of relief. "I'm fine, I'm fine," he told her. Then he addressed the others, as well, as they reached him: "So, we made it through a long night. And the daylight chases away the shadows." Even as King Adam spoke, the rain slowed, and the room lightened around them.

"But what happened here?" asked Calderon.

"Are you sure you're all right, my king?" asked Anna, still worried.

And Sara quickly added, "King Landon and the others showed up to the fight, your highness, but when you didn't, I was concerned."

They had all spoken nearly at once, and King Adam smiled. "For now, healing and repairing are most important, but the other leaders are safe, at least. Nothing would hold back my fellow leaders from a good fight. Now, we all should see that everything that needs to be done is done."

An hour later, after helping King Landon repair some of the damaged walls, Sara and some other dwarves worked on initial repairs to the castle's structure. Calderon was in his bed, where healers could treat his wounds. King Landon, King Adam, and his friends had ordered him to rest and stay put while being tended to. He had agreed after King Adam had said he would get his daughter after him. Julia, the king told Calderon, had been with the guards at the wall. Why she had been at the wall, Calderon didn't know, but it was good she had come through the fight unharmed.

Soon, a Dwelling Elf girl came in. She wore the white robe of a healer. She had pretty grey eyes and dark brown hair that was cropped short. Her face was heart-shaped, and Calderon smiled despite how he felt.

"Just drink this, young master, and sleep," she said, giving him a warm smile.

Calderon took the flask she held out to him, which was full of a dark blue liquid. Without thinking, he drank it in one draft. Then, lying back on his pillow, he found sleep quickly stealing over him.

However, he asked drowsily, "How are things going? Are many injured?"

The healer moved closer to him, laying one comforting hand on his forehead and checking his bandages with the other. "Not as many as there could have been. Now, rest. I'm going to change your bandages and get food for when you wake up."

Calderon thought dreamily to ask who she was, but he felt like he was falling backwards, and then he was fast asleep.

When he woke up, someone was sitting on his bed. It was King Adam, who held a mug of something steaming. Seeing Calderon was awake, he smiled and offered him the mug. Calderon took a careful sip and felt himself warm up from the drink. It was hot apple cider.

"Thank you, your highness. How are things?" Calderon asked, handing the mug back to King Adam.

"Everything is going very well. Don't worry. I've heard about the fight in the library and how you led the defense of the castle. I can give no higher praise than to say your parents would be proud of you."

Calderon smiled and felt his eyes brimming with tears. He looked away hurriedly and rubbed his eyes, hoping the King hadn't seen.

Then, looking back at King Adam, he said, "But Prince Elian and Krasp—they got away."

King Adam nodded and smiled as though it didn't bother him. "For now, all that matters is we withstood whatever plot they had devised for last night. You survived and kept the Dragon's Tooth from falling into their hands. And not just that, but the enemy is now out in the open and we know who they are."

Calderon nodded, "Yeah. Krasp and Elian."

King Adam frowned, saying sadly, "No, it's much worse than that."

The king took a deep breath, and Calderon felt a foreboding. "What could be worse?" he asked.

Meeting his eye, King Adam said solemnly, "Now more than ever, we need the support of all the races. You must get the other piece of the Dragon's Tooth and return it to its true form. The Dark Elves have returned."

About the Author

Growing up in the heartland of Missouri, author Benjamin Coward first discovered the thrill of world-building through role-playing games like Dungeons and Dragons and books in The Inheritance Cycle series by Christopher Paolini. In his debut YA fantasy novel, Benjamin masterfully creates a realm where relatable characters fight evil opponents and overcome struggles through teamwork and self-trust. With a bachelor's degree in environmental science and now living and working in north central Florida, Benjamin's love of nature and history often seep into his storytelling, enriching the fantastical worlds he creates.

www.ingramcontent.com/pod-product-compliance
Lightning Source LLC
Chambersburg PA
CBHW051436130726
47987CB00005B/2080